HOME WITH YOU

THE SAN DIEGO MARINES, BOOK SIX

JESS MASTORAKOS

To get a free copy of the prequel, Forever with You, visit: http://jessmastorakos.com/forever-with-you

1

OWEN

"Okay, bud," I said, reaching down to rustle Finn's hair as we closed the door behind us. "Last chance. Are you sure you don't want to stay home with Grandma?"

Finn shook his head, a wide grin on his face. "No way. I want to meet my uncle."

I nodded and swallowed back the worry threatening to break free as I smiled at my son. There was a noticeable pep in his step as we walked down our driveway in the military housing neighborhood. We'd only moved to San Diego from South Carolina a week earlier. Once I'd found out I had a half-brother who was also a Marine stationed at Miramar, I'd wasted no time in tracking him down. I couldn't believe my eyes when I saw how close he lived with his wife. They were right down the street.

Nerves swam in my gut. I had no idea what they would be like. With the little I knew about the father we share, I had no frame of reference. He could be great. He could be everything I'd ever dreamed of having in a brother. Or, he could be a total tool. He could slam the door in my face and call me a freak for looking him up out of the blue like this. I shuddered at the thought. What would Finn think if that happened? How would I explain that to an eight-year-old?

Finn grabbed my hand. "Relax, Dad."

Unsurprised that he'd picked up on my nervous energy, I blew out a breath. "Sorry."

"He's gonna love us. It'll be great."

"I'm sure it will." I gave him what I hoped was an excited smile.

His deep-brown eyes widened and he leaned back, wrinkling his nose and laughing. "Now you look scary. Don't smile at Uncle Spencer like that."

I laughed and pulled him close to my side. "I'll try not to."

Glancing up at the clear, blue sky, I sent a prayer up that *Uncle Spencer* wouldn't say something to hurt my kid. He'd had plenty of hurt in his short life and not enough family. Hence why he was so excited to meet a new relative. *Dear God, please let him be as cool as Finn hopes he is.* I wasn't sure if I could handle seeing the disappointed look on his face after everything he'd been through.

I'd planned to keep my half-brother's existence a secret from Finn until I knew if he'd be a good influence. But, as usual, the little sneak was hiding behind the couch when I'd been talking about it with my mom. At that point, I'd had to explain everything. Truth be told, it was a weight lifted off my shoulders. We'd been through a lot and I didn't like keeping anything from him. But now, as we headed over to meet the guy, that same weight felt like it was pressing down on my chest. Had I made a mistake?

Finn had been reciting an episode of *Ben 10: Omniverse* word for word as we walked, and I'd tuned back in just in time to hear him ask if I could believe that they were traveling through time and not through *universes* like they usually did.

"Oh, man," I replied, wrinkling my brow like I was blown away. "That is *wild*."

"I know. That was the last episode of the whole series, too."

"What are you going to watch now?"

"I'm going to go back to the beginning and watch it again," he said, his tone matter-of-fact.

"All of it? Even the filler episodes?" I remembered

him skipping those in an anime show he liked, though the name of it always escaped me.

"Yes, because I can't skip that many filler episodes. They start after the Incurseans come and last forever. I still like them."

"What's an Incursean?"

He looked at me like I should know this, then sighed. "A frog alien."

"Right, sorry." I scratched my head, finding myself out of my depth with his interests. Again.

"Hey, is this it?" Finn asked excitedly, pointing up at the townhome on our right.

I balked, looking back the way we came and spotting our house in the distance. "Wow, yeah. That was a quick walk."

"I can't believe he lives so close," Finn exclaimed.

I'd been thinking the same thing, but with more of a nervous lean to it. "Yep."

He ran to the door before I could stop him and eagerly pressed the bell. I jogged up the driveway and got to his side just as the door opened, revealing a pretty blonde in a bright sundress standing behind the screen door.

"Hi," she greeted us, a warm smile for Finn before her gaze turned to me. "Can I help you?"

"Hi," Finn said, opening his mouth to say more, but

it came out muffled as I placed my hand over his mouth.

"Hi," I said, smiling tightly. "We're here to see Spencer. Is he around?"

She chuckled and nodded. "Yeah, one sec, I'll go grab him."

"Thanks."

Finn pulled my hand off his mouth and glared up at me after she left. "I was going to ask if she's my aunt."

"I *know*," I whispered. "Keep your cool, little dude. We don't want to scare them."

A moment later, the door opened wider and a young guy stepped up to the screen. His hand hovered over the door handle for a moment as he looked at me and then at Finn. When his eyes—the same eyes I knew I had—traveled back to mine, the recognition in them was apparent. Looking at him was like looking at myself, but a handful of years younger. The resemblance between us was solid. Immediately, I figured our shared father must look a lot like us too, and it made me even more nervous to meet him.

He shook his head as if to clear it, probably freaked out by the similarities between us. He pushed open the screen door and stepped onto the porch. "Who *are* you?"

His wife—or at least, the girl I assumed was his wife —sucked in a breath. "Spence."

"No," I said, holding up a hand. It made total sense that he'd be a bit confused by us standing here, showing up out of the blue. Especially since the family resemblance was strong. "It's okay. I'm uh ... well, we're ..."

"You guys are brothers," Finn supplied when my words failed me.

"Right," I said, resting a hand on his shoulder. "What he said. Well, *half*-brothers."

Almost as if he'd expected there to be some explanation for our shared blue eyes, blond hair, and height, Spencer nodded once and crossed his arms over his chest. He tilted his head at Finn. Then he looked back at me. Then down at Finn again. His face was blank, but I could tell he was doing a lot of thinking. Finally, his gaze landed on his girl. She gave him a small smile and nod, and even though I didn't know them, I could see years of trust and love between them. My heart squeezed. I knew what it felt like to have what they seemed to have. And even though I didn't know him, he was still my blood. And it made me happy to see he'd found what I once had.

Spencer turned back to me and cleared his throat, a smile tugging up the corner of his mouth. "You look like my dad. I could see it right away."

Relief washed over me. If he was about to slam the door in our faces, he probably wouldn't start with that.

"You guys look a lot like each other, too," the girl beside him chimed in, her eyes flicking between us.

Finn bounced up and down, a wide smile for his uncle. "Can you tell us about him? About your dad, I mean? He was a Marine too, right? Like you guys? Is that why you're a Marine?"

"Easy, Finn," I said, squeezing his shoulder slightly. "Just breathe, buddy."

"Uh, sure, I can tell you about him," Spencer said, chuckling and bending down to get eye-level with my son. "If *he's* my brother, what does that make you?"

"Your nephew." Finn straightened his shoulders.

Spencer smiled. "I've always wanted a nephew."

"I've always wanted an uncle," Finn asserted. Then his gaze traveled to the girl in the doorway, her hand over her mouth. "Is she my aunt?"

Spencer straightened and held out a hand for her. "Sorry, yeah, this is my wife."

"Ellie," she said, stepping forward and shaking my hand, and then Finn's. "Nice to meet you both."

"It's nice to meet you, too," I said. "Sorry to barge in on you guys. I hope we're not interrupting."

Ellie waved a hand. "It's totally fine. Why don't you guys come in and hang out? We're having a going away party for one of our friends."

"We'd love to," Finn piped up.

"Actually, do you want to take a walk so we can talk?

There's a playground over there," Spencer asked me, and I nodded. He kissed Ellie on the cheek. "You can tell the others I stepped out, right babe?"

"Yeah, of course," she replied, heading for the door again. "Take your time."

We said our goodbyes and headed down the driveway. Again, I felt Finn buzzing with energy beside me.

"So, tell us about my grandpa," Finn said.

Spencer made a face. "Oh, man. *Grandpa.*"

"Yeah," Finn said, rolling his eyes and pointing at me. "Because I'm *his* kid, and he's *your dad's* kid. So your dad is my grandpa."

With a laugh, Spencer looked at me, and I shrugged.

"Guess so," Spencer allowed. "What are your names? Sorry, I'm still a little blown away over here. I didn't catch them."

Realizing how dumb it was that I hadn't even introduced us, I let out a breath and held out my hand for him to shake. "Sorry, man. I'm Owen O'Malley. This is my son, Finn."

"And you're Spencer, aka *Uncle* Spencer to me," Finn said. "And your dad is Mike, aka Grandpa."

"Right," Spencer said as we walked, leading us down a sidewalk toward the playground at the end of the row houses. "Man, this is nuts. I'm dying to hear how all of this came out."

"Oh, I can tell you that," Finn offered. "First, my dad got orders to San Diego."

"You're a Marine, too, then?" Spencer asked me.

"Yep, I'm in air traffic control," I replied.

"Cool."

"And when he told my grandma that we were moving here," Finn continued, "Grandma got super weird. Like *really* weird. All twitchy and stuff."

I chuckled, remembering my mom's reaction when she'd heard the news. As a rule, she was a very calm woman. She didn't let things get her down, had a strong faith, and was rarely frazzled. One of those *everything happens according to God's plan, don't sweat the small stuff* types. Seeing her all "twitchy" was a rare sight.

"But they didn't tell me anything," Finn went on, "so I was really confused. I thought she didn't want to leave South Carolina. She lives with us."

"We tried to keep it on the down low, but this little special agent hears everything," I said, nudging Finn with my elbow. "After he went to bed that night, my mom told me San Diego was where my dad had gone when he'd left combat training. Obviously, that was a long time ago, but still. It hit a nerve for her."

Spencer looked up like he was trying to connect dots in his head. "Okay, combat training. Dad went to SOI-East for combat training. So did your mom live near Camp Geiger?"

"Yep," I replied. "He was about to head to Pendleton for his first duty station. She was a server at an off-base sports bar. He went in to blow off some steam the night before he left, and the rest is history."

"Ah," Spencer said, connecting the dots of what must have happened that night between our father and my mother.

We'd reached the playground and Finn tugged on my arm. "Can I go swing?"

"Yeah, go for it," I said. "Stay where I can see you."

"Okay," Finn hollered behind him as he ran for the swings. I watched him for a minute to make sure he got settled before turning back to Spencer. "He's eight."

Spencer nodded. "He seems really cool."

"He is," I confirmed. "Coolest kid I know."

"So," Spencer said, clapping his hands and rubbing them together. "If I'm counting right, that would make you about six years older than me?"

I shrugged. "If you say so."

"And, uh, sorry if this is weird but ... did they not exchange phone numbers? Did she never tell him she was pregnant? I can't imagine my dad would know about you and not ... like, *be there*. You know?"

"She's really not proud of this, but she only knew his first name. Mike. And that he'd just finished combat training and was about to move to San Diego. Not much to go on since she didn't even know which base he was going to. It could have been Miramar or Pendleton."

Spencer snickered. "It was Pendleton, which is a huge base anyway. And Mike isn't exactly a unique name."

"Right."

"My dad—er, our dad, I guess—was no angel, either. He joined the Marines because the judge said it was either that or jail. I guess that was a thing back then."

"I see," I said, not loving the picture he painted of the man I'd grown up wondering about.

I'd spent countless nights lying awake in bed thinking about my dad. My mom had always been honest with me about how little she knew about him, and that left a lot of room to imagine what he was like. Sometimes I'd pictured him as a nice, blue-collar guy who got out of the Marines and became a mechanic. He had a pretty wife and a bunch of other kids, and if he'd known about me, he would have welcomed me and my mom into his life with open arms.

Other times I pictured him as a bad guy. Got kicked out of the Marines, couldn't hold a job, and wouldn't be the kind of dude my mom would want me to know anyway. When I thought of him like that, I told myself I was better off with only my mom. It helped sometimes.

The versions I imagined of my dad always swung

from one end of the spectrum to the other, with no in-between. I was inexplicably bummed out that he sounded like the bad version.

Spencer waved a hand. "It worked out though, he wound up turning his life around and making a career out of it. He retired as a master sergeant."

My chest swelled. He was the good guy. "Wow. And he and your mom ..."

"They were married," Spencer rubbed the back of his neck. "She died when I was twelve."

"Aw, man. I'm so sorry." A buried part of me, the part who had to watch my son deal with that kind of pain, threatened to surface. I had a lot of practice squashing it, but this day was already doing a number on my nerves and it was harder than normal.

"Thanks. Anyway, so, okay. My dad hooked up with your mom, and then she didn't know how to get ahold of him. Did you decide to track him down when you found out you were moving here?"

"Pretty much, yeah. A buddy suggested one of those mail-in DNA tests. He said he'd seen on the news how people were finding their long-lost relatives with it. I knew it was a long shot because if he hadn't taken the test, he wouldn't show up. But I figured I might be able to find some other family member."

Spencer nodded. "Ah-ha. That makes sense. Ellie and I took it last year when they had a two-for-one deal.

Thought it would be cool to look into our ancestors and stuff. Didn't see anything about a long-lost brother, though."

"Probably because I hadn't taken the test yet."

"Right." Spencer stuffed his hands in his pockets and blew out a breath.

"I know this is a lot," I offered, keeping my eyes on Finn as he swung back and forth on the swing set.

"Nah—I mean, yeah, it is, but it's also pretty cool."

Relief filled me again and I felt like I was on a roller coaster. I cleared my throat. "Do you have any brothers or sisters?"

"Nope. It's just me. I wasn't lying earlier when I said I've always wanted a nephew. I've always wanted siblings and a big family. Ellie and I are both only children so we don't really have a lot of family. Did your mom have more kids? Did you grow up with a stepdad?"

I shook my head. "No, my mom never married, no more kids. It was only the two of us."

"Your son—what was his name? Sorry."

"Finn."

"Thanks, yeah, Finn said your mom lived with you. So it's you, your mom, Finn, and your wife?"

I swallowed. "My uh ... Rebecca, my wife, passed away about three years ago. Hodgkin's lymphoma."

The look on Spencer's face at that moment could

only be described as *knowing*. I'd talked to many people while my wife was sick and then after she died, and the look in their eyes right after I told them about Rebecca always told me how the rest of the conversation would go. If they'd never experienced a loss at this level, it was pity. It was distant sadness. It was the embodiment of the phrase "I couldn't imagine."

I know people meant well, so I handled it better now than I used to. After Rebecca first got sick, and I was constantly living with the fear of her diagnosis and potentially losing her, I seethed with rage every time someone looked at me with that pitying expression. I found myself wanting to literally slap it off their face. It was completely outrageous and unhealthy, and it took me a long time to stop feeling that way. The only things that helped me go from anger to acceptance were God, time, and my need to be a good example for Finn. I was all he had.

The alternative to the pitying look was the expression Spencer now wore. It was the look of someone who knew our pain and knew it was so deep that a moment of silence and a simple "I'm sorry" were enough. More words didn't make anything better.

"I'm sorry," he said, his words sliding into place like pieces of a puzzle.

"Thank you. My mom moved in to help us when

Rebecca first got sick and then stayed after she passed to help me with Finn."

I watched as his gaze locked on Finn. I knew he must be thinking about the loss they shared. "How's he doing with it?"

I swallowed the lump in my throat. "He had a lot of time to process that she was sick. She was always really open with him about how she might not get better. I hated it so much at the time."

"My mom was the same way with me. I remember it making my dad uncomfortable."

Guilt crept up the back of my neck. I hoped beyond hope that I hadn't done anything to show Finn how much I'd hated it. I didn't know if those were good memories of his mom or not, but I prayed my own emotional response hadn't put a stain on them or anything. On the other hand, Spencer had been twelve when his mom died, not five. Maybe he remembered more than Finn would. Which had its good and bad points.

"I can see now that it helped him let her go, in a way. He was sad, obviously. But he wasn't confused about it. He saw her get sicker and sicker. The first year was the worst, but it gets better each year, I guess."

Spencer's eyes held mine. "It'll keep getting better. Don't worry."

"Thanks."

"And, uh, if you think he might want to talk about it, let me know. I'm not promising to know exactly what to say, but I might be able to help a little."

I nodded in reply, not trusting myself to speak. A lot of scenarios went through my mind leading up to this day. Finding that my half-brother had lost his mom as a kid, and might be able to give Finn some comfort in that area, blew my mind. Yep, my ability to hold my bearing was slipping *fast*.

Spencer shuddered as if he were trying to shake off his own emotions, then chuckled. "Back to the story. You saw my name on the DNA test results and then used your super stalker skills to find my address?"

"Pretty much," I replied with a laugh. "First I Googled you. Then I saw on your social media profile that you were a Marine. It was easy from there."

"MOL." Spencer made a clicking sound with his mouth and pointed a finger, correctly guessing that I'd used Marine Online, the database Marines used for all kinds of administrative tasks. One of its many features was that you could look people up if they were a former or current Marine, then find out where they were stationed and with what unit.

"Yep."

Finn ran up to us then, out of breath. "Do you and Aunt Ellie want to come over for dinner? My grandma is a great cook."

I laughed and ran a hand over the back of my neck. "Finn."

Again, Spencer bent to Finn's level. "We would love to come over for dinner. Pick a day, and we'll be there."

"Tomorrow?"

"Tomorrow it is." Spencer held his hand out for a high five. An overjoyed Finn slapped it as hard as he could, then bubbled up with laughter as Spencer feigned a wounded hand.

2

RACHEL

I'd always heard that when you love what you do, you don't work a day in your life. As a physical education teacher at an elementary school, I'd found that to be true. I felt right at home with the stinky, sweaty, and rambunctious kids. I loved that my class gave them permission to get their sillies out and burn off the energy they'd been saving up all day. Unlike my sweet friends who taught math or English, my kids rushed into class with big smiles and anticipation.

Well, many of them did. There were always the few who dreaded my class and preferred math or English. I could spot them right away. Their eyes darted around, hoping they wouldn't need to do anything particularly athletic that day. They prayed for free play because then they could try to blend in with the rest of the kids and do nothing. Honestly, I respected their feelings about PE. Being in education meant I was well versed in different learning styles and personality types. But at the end of the day, my job was to help kids learn how to live a happy, healthy, and active lifestyle. And I wanted to do that job by helping *everyone* have fun. Especially the ones who didn't want to.

Finn O'Malley was one of them. From the moment he stepped into the gym, I could tell. And just like every student I'd had in the last seven years in this role, I wanted nothing more than to be his friend, show him that being active could be fun, and not make him feel like he was being bullied into exercising.

I bent to his eye level, hands on my knees, the whistle around my neck swinging between us. "Hey, Finn, welcome to PE. I'm Ms. Peters."

He pursed his lips. "Hi."

We were only a week into the new school year so most of the kids were still getting the hang of their new routines. I'd never taught at a school on base before, but I'd been warned that I'd lose some students throughout the year as their parents got transferred to other bases. I was nervous about it since my prior experience was at a public school and I was used to knowing my students for years. I was sure I'd be sad to see them go.

On the flip side, I also knew I'd gain students

throughout the year as their parents transferred. Finn had only missed the first week of school, and in my opinion, this probably made it a lot easier on him to transition, since the other kids hadn't gotten too far into the groove yet.

"Where did you move from?" I smiled at him, then did a quick sweep of the room with my eyes to check on the rest of the class. They were happily rolling around on scooter boards and maneuvering through the track I'd made on the floor out of colorful masking tape.

"Beaufort, South Carolina," he replied matter-of-factly, his quiet voice barely audible over the commotion in the gym.

"Wow, you've come a long way. Do you like San Diego so far?"

Finn shrugged. "I guess. I haven't seen much yet."

"Have you gone to the beach yet?"

He shook his head.

"I'm new to San Diego, too," I said, "and I can tell you the beach is definitely worth a trip."

"You're new here, too?" he asked, the first glimmer of interest appearing in his eyes.

I nodded. "Yep! Just moved here right before the school year started. It's kind of scary moving to a new place, don't you think?"

"Kinda."

"Maybe we can talk to each other about it and it'll help us be more excited about our new home."

"Maybe." He bit his lip and looked over at the kids on their scooter boards. Then his gaze met mine. "Where did you move from?"

"Fort Worth, Texas."

He looked at my feet. "Do you normally wear cowboy boots? When you're not being a PE teacher, of course."

A wide grin spread over my face and I wrinkled my nose. "I usually stick to my running shoes. And when I'm not wearing these, I'm more of a flip-flop kinda gal."

"Oh, okay."

With a tilt of my head, I gestured to the other kids rolling around on scooter boards. "Have you ever tried riding on one of those bad boys?"

He nodded grimly. "Once. It did *not* go well."

"Wanna tell me about it?"

"Not really."

This kid was going to be a tough nut to crack. But I'd keep trying. "Ah, come on. I'm a great listener."

He narrowed his eyes at me. "Fine. One time, at my old school, we were told to pick a color and grab a board. This kid Max—who I *really* didn't like—grabbed my blue board out of my hand. I had to use a red one, even though that's not my favorite color. Then, even though I was following the course and trying to stay in the lines and do what we were supposed to do, there were kids all over the place running into each other and not following directions. It was total chaos. I just wanted to beat the level, or course, or whatever. You know?"

I nodded, my face reflecting an appropriate level of concern and understanding. "Yeah, of course. That would be really frustrating. I'm like you, once I understand the rules of a game, I like to follow them."

"I don't like it when people go wherever they want. See, like that kid. *Don't look.* He's all over the place. Not following the lines at all."

"Yes, totally." I smiled to myself but my face remained solemn to match his.

Finn didn't know it, but he'd just given me a huge gift. Now I knew part of what made him tick when it came to games and sports. He liked rules. He liked to pay attention to detail. And since he'd referred to the course as a *level*, I could tell video games were a big part of his life. With kids like Finn, I had to appeal to the things they liked, and it made them more excited about being active. I enjoyed the challenge of showing them that they could like both virtual *and* physical games.

"Obviously," Finn continued, "with everyone going all over the place and not paying attention to the track, I fell off my board and crashed and stuff. It was *not* fun."

"That doesn't sound fun. You're right," I said, then cupped my hands over my mouth and hollered across the room. "Daniel, if you can't play fair, you don't get to play! Consider this your first warning."

Finn crossed his arms next to me. "Seems like he's going to be another Max."

My heart squeezed for him. Most kids fell in the middle of the spectrum when it came to how they reacted to rough play. On one end, there were the kids like Daniel—and apparently, Max—who loved to get down and dirty. They could take a tumble and bounce up like it didn't even happen. In fact, sometimes they'd call attention to it and ask if their friends saw their "epic wipeout."

And then at the other end, where Finn seemed to land, falling was embarrassing, scary, and something they avoided at all costs. It was hard to get these kids to run fast and play hard when they were always worried about getting hurt or making a fool out of themselves. But that wouldn't stop me from trying, of course.

"Tell you what." I crossed my arms over my chest. "How about you head over to the carts and grab yourself a blue board?"

He turned to look at the carts, his brows lifting as he registered that there was only one color, blue. He looked back at the gym floor in front of us and noticed the kids zooming around the track, each of them on blue boards.

He turned back to me. "Seems like a good way to avoid fighting over the colors."

I hadn't chosen what color boards to get, but I nodded. "Definitely. Now, I've been watching the class while we've been talking, and I think everyone is doing a pretty good job following the course and not going all over the place. But, if it will make you feel more comfortable, I'll make an announcement to remind them."

Finn balked. "No, thank you. They'll know you're only saying something about it because I said something about it to you."

For an eight-year-old, this kid was quite an advanced thinker. His speech and verbal communication skills were advanced, too. I had a feeling he did great in academic classes. "Okay, I won't make an announcement. But I will make sure to correct anyone I see not following the rules of the game. I want you to be able to get out there and have some fun."

"It's pretty fun talking to you."

My heart swelled. "I'm having fun talking to you, too. But this class is all about having an active lifestyle. So grab a board, start at the beginning, and see if you can work your way through the course without getting eaten by a giant Pac-Man."

He jolted. "What?"

"You know, like the little chomping yellow guy?" I opened and closed my hand like a mouth, chomping the air between us and making him laugh.

Finn rolled his eyes. "You're funny. Fine, I'll go grab a board."

"Thank you. You'll have fun, I *promise*."

"We'll see," he called over his shoulder as he ran for the carts.

Three hours later, I slung the strap of my duffel bag over my shoulder and headed out of the gym. I breathed in the fresh air as I made my way to the teacher's parking lot. I had a special ID card to work as a civilian on a military base, but I sure wished I was able to live there, too. I saw all of the families walking to and from school every day, and as nice as the weather was in San Diego, it made me yearn to do the same. In Fort Worth, there were times of the year that you would *not* want to do that. But here? Shoot. If it stayed this nice all year long, I might start sleeping in a hammock outside.

"Mrs. Peters," a young voice called, causing me to look around despite his use of *Mrs.* instead of *Ms.* "Mrs. Peters, over here!"

I turned to find Finn standing with an older woman. "Oh, hey, Finn."

"This is my grandma," he called as I got closer.

"Hi, I'm Diane," the woman said, holding her hand out for me to shake. "Finn was just telling me how much *fun* he had in PE today."

I couldn't miss the look of surprise on her face as she said the words. "Ah, yes. We had a blast on the scooter boards today, huh?"

Finn nodded. "Yes. It was the *best*."

"I'm so glad, sweetheart. Your dad is going to be thrilled to hear it," Diane said, beaming at her grandson. Then she turned to me. "Normally our Finn isn't a big fan of PE."

I waved a hand. "Oh, I think that's because he hadn't had me for a PE teacher yet. Right, Finn?"

"Right," he agreed. Then he looked up at his grandma. "Don't tell Dad, though. He'll get his hopes up and try to sign me up for baseball or something."

I reached into the pocket of my workout leggings and pulled out a flyer, unfolding it and handing it to Finn. "I actually signed up to coach. Would you do it if you could be on my team?"

Finn looked at the paper, bit his lip, then folded it and handed it back. "No, thanks."

"Okay. Worth a shot." I rustled his hair. "I'll see you tomorrow, Finn. Nice to meet you, Diane."

"Nice to meet you too, Mrs. Peters," she replied as Finn waved.

I turned to leave, trying to ignore the fact that I was starting yet another school year as *Ms.* Peters instead of Mrs. Whatever-Else. Sure, I didn't want to marry just anybody for the sake of getting married. But in a world where parents and kids constantly said *Mrs.* instead of *Ms.,* I knew I'd be happy when one day it wouldn't be a mistake. I really needed to stop striking out in the dating department.

Pulling out my phone, I sent a quick text to Ellie.

Me: Hey, do you want to have a girl's night this weekend? Maybe we can go dancing or something?

The thought bubble that indicated she was replying showed up, so I paused on the sidewalk for her response. Eager kids rushed past me, excited for their after-school freedom.

Ellie: Yeah, maybe! I'll talk to Spencer and let you know.

I cringed and slipped my phone in my pocket. My girlfriends here in San Diego were awesome. I'd met them through my old roommate, Ivy, and I was so grateful for how they'd pulled me right into their tight-knit group of friends. The only problem was, they were all happily coupled up. Here I was trying to go out on the town and find my Prince Charming, and Ellie had to check with hers before she committed.

Sighing, I hopped into the front seat of my open-air Jeep and turned the key. Maybe a bar wasn't the best place to find Prince Charming, anyway.

3

OWEN

"Hey, man," Spencer greeted me as he opened the front door. "Thanks for coming. No Finn?"

I shook my head and followed him into the kitchen. "I thought it might be better to surprise him with one thing at a time. Finding out he has another son is one thing, I'd rather see his reaction to *that* before he finds out he's a grandpa, too."

"Yeah, I get that. Finn's great though, man. Don't sweat it." Spencer handed me a cold drink from the fridge without even asking if I wanted one. It made me feel at home, but I also wondered if it meant he was a little nervous.

"So, thanks again for offering to host this little meet

and greet. Are you planning to stick around so we can tell him together?"

Spencer held out his hands. "That's up to you. Ellie's at a friend's house, so it's just us, but if you want me to hang out in another room while you talk to him, that's cool with me."

"Nah. I mean, it's okay with me if you're there. Might be good to have another person there in case it gets weird. You know him ... do you think he's gonna freak out?"

"Probably. I know I would. Wouldn't you?"

I chuckled. "Yeah, I guess so."

"Listen, Mike Hawkins isn't a man of many words."

Hearing his full name for the first time gave me a jolt. I'd figured that was his last name since *Spencer Hawkins* was the name on the DNA match, but still. It was the first time in my entire life I'd heard someone refer to my father by his full name.

"He doesn't like feelings very much either," Spencer went on. "I bet this'll be a pretty straightforward conversation. And then before it gets weird, I can tell him we have plans with friends and have to go. He'll probably be pretty grateful for the excuse to escape. He's the type to process in his own head, in his own time, you know?"

Being that exact type of guy myself, I raised a brow. "I think I have some idea."

"And you should actually come, by the way."

"Where?"

"To my friend's house. My buddy is having everyone over for the fantasy football draft."

I scratched my head. "Are these the same friends who were over at your place the other day when we met?"

"Sort of. That was a going away party for Brooks and Cat. He's a warrant officer now and they just got stationed at Lejeune. But everyone else who was there will be at the fantasy draft. We get together a lot actually. It's mostly couples. Well, except for Noah. Oh, and Rachel. They're kind of new to the group. That's how it is with military friends though, right? People are always coming in and out."

"Yeah, no doubt." I was no stranger to friends coming and going. I'd had plenty of friends over the years who'd gotten stationed in a new place and moved away. I was also pretty used to being one of the only single guys in a group of couples. All of my friends back East were married with kids. Speaking of, I was eager to find a new friend for Finn. Preferably one who liked to hang out outside and play ball. He needed some of that in his life. "Do any of your friends have kids Finn's age?"

Spencer shook his head. "Nah, sorry. The only kid in the group is my goddaughter, Amelia, but she's a toddler."

"What about you guys? Do you and Ellie want kids someday?"

"Yeah, we do. Ellie's pretty eager now that two of our friends have headed down that road. Amelia is Mills's daughter, and Brooks and Cat just told us they're pregnant at the going away party. So, we'll see when it happens for us. I'm not trying to stress about it. I've heard it can be kind of a bummer if you make it stressful."

"True." I laughed, remembering my own experience when we were trying for Finn.

Rebecca and I tried not to get disappointed when it didn't happen as quickly as we'd hoped, but that was probably normal. I made a mental note to check in with him in the coming months in order to make sure he wasn't getting into his head about it. I remember thinking how there had to be something wrong with me a time or two when really it was just God's timing, as my mom would say. I shook my head and jammed my hands into my pockets. I barely knew Spencer and here I was, making plans to give him pep talks about having a kid.

There was a knock at the door, and we looked at each other. My heart rate took off, and I could practically feel the blood pumping through my body. I couldn't remember a time in my life when I hadn't wondered about my dad. As nervous as I'd been to meet

Spencer, I hadn't known he existed for very long, so it wasn't nearly the same thing.

Spencer patted me on the shoulder as he passed by, then opened the door, revealing a tall man with an athletic build and a shaved head. He and Spencer resembled each other a lot, and I saw the same set of eyes I was so familiar with staring back at me when he walked through the door. Mike greeted Spencer, but his gaze didn't leave my face.

"Dad," Spencer said, looking between us. "This is Owen."

Mike stepped forward and extended his hand toward me. I hesitated for only a moment before taking it and giving it a firm shake. Ice floated around in my gut, threatening to make me sick. Here he was, right in front of me, in the flesh. He was right in front of me and shaking my hand. He wasn't long dead. Or a convict. Or impossible to find. He was here.

"Owen," Mike said, his voice gravelly and unfamiliar. "Nice to meet you."

"You, too," I said, my hand still in his.

He analyzed my face with a furrowed brow, glancing back and forth between me and Spencer. "Have we met?"

Spencer cleared his throat and I shook my head. "No, sir."

"You look ... *familiar*."

"Dad, let's go have a seat and talk." Spencer put a hand on Mike's shoulder and led us into his living room.

My mind raced. I'd prepared for this moment my whole life. And yet, the words were stuck in my throat, just like they had been the day I'd met my half-brother. I swallowed, attempting to dislodge the right thing to say and leave all of the gibberish behind.

"I'm your son," I blurted.

Mike's butt hadn't even hit the couch, and he dropped into the seat like he'd had his legs ripped out from under him. "My what?"

"Your son."

Spencer's face contorted into a surprised grimace as he watched.

Mike leaned forward, resting his elbows on his knees, and stared at me from across the coffee table. "You're my *son*."

I nodded, unable to say more.

His eyes searched my face for any sign that I was lying. Then he turned to Spencer. "What do you know about this?"

"It's true, Dad. He showed me the DNA test that listed me as his half-brother."

"DNA test?" he asked. "You mean that test you and Ellie took last year? That didn't say anything about a half-brother."

"That's because he hadn't taken it yet. Once he did, since I was in the system, I popped up for him," Spencer explained.

I was grateful he was there. His explanations gave me time to process and let the shock wear off so I could form coherent sentences.

"Okay, let's back up," Mike said, turning back to me. "Your name is Owen? Owen, what?"

"O'Malley," I replied.

His eyes traveled to the ceiling, and he tilted his head like he was thinking. "O'Malley? I can't ... how old are you?"

"Thirty-one."

His eyes bulged. "I would have been ... so you ... is your mom ..."

I waited. I didn't fill in his thoughts, because I wanted to hear if he remembered her. I needed to know if she was a blip on his radar or if he'd ever thought about her again. The protectiveness I felt for her was at war with a deep-seated yearning to know him. I prayed that he wouldn't say anything about her that would make me want to punch him. That was not the road I wanted to travel down today.

"Is your mom *Diane*?"

Spencer and I looked at each other with wide eyes, and I turned back to Mike, trying to swallow back the emotions coursing through me. "Yeah, Diane O'Malley."

Mike sat back and heaved out a sigh. "Diane O'Malley. I'll be."

I leaned forward. "You remember her?"

"Remember her?" he scoffed. "Sure, I do. She worked at a bar off base when I was in combat training at Camp Geiger. Took me a few times of going in there to get up the nerve to talk to her. When I finally did, it was my last night in town. Headed to Camp Pendleton the next day."

"Your first time talking to her resulted in ... *him*?" Spencer asked, swinging a long arm in my direction.

Mike ran a hand over his shiny head. "Yeah, well, we hit it off."

I forced those thoughts away, considering it was my mom we were talking about, and focused on the questions I'd always wanted to ask. "You didn't try to look her up afterward?"

"Actually, I did. I called the bar a few weeks later looking for her. I didn't know anything but her first name. I found a matchbox in my seabag with the bar's phone number on it and I gave it a shot. The guy who answered the phone said she'd quit and wouldn't give me her number."

My face felt hot. "She quit right after she found out

she was pregnant. Didn't want to work in a bar with all the smoke because it made her feel sick."

Mike frowned. "She must have made you grow up hating me. I swear, kid. I didn't know ... if I'd known ..."

"You would've gone to her. And you wouldn't have met and married Mom," Spencer said quietly from beside him, looking at his hands.

Mike reached over and grabbed the back of Spencer's neck, giving it a gentle squeeze. He didn't disagree with that statement, but he probably didn't want to confirm it out loud to the son he'd raised.

"She didn't raise me up to hate you," I finally said. "Once I was old enough to understand, she let me know that you guys didn't have any way to find each other. A Marine named Mike, who at one point moved to San Diego, wasn't much to go on. She said she tried. She didn't even know the name of the base you were going to, just the city you were flying into."

He nodded. "And I didn't know where to look once calling the bar didn't pan out. I would have tried harder if I'd known I had such a big reason. How is she now? Does she know you're here? Does she know you found us?"

"She's great," I replied. "She's the one who encouraged me to find you once I found out I was getting stationed here."

"Stationed? You're in the military?"

I nodded. "A Marine. Staff sergeant, air traffic control."

"A Marine." He looked between me and Spencer with a small smile.

I wondered if it made him happy that both of his sons had followed in his footsteps even if he hadn't had a direct hand in my upbringing. He ran both of his hands over his face and sat there for a moment, breathing heavily through the small space between his hands. I fidgeted with the corner of my nail, not sure if I should say anything or let him take it all in. I glanced at Spencer, and he gave me a nod of encouragement.

"I have a son," I offered quietly.

Mike's head popped up, and his eyes swam with emotion. "A son?"

"His name is Finn. He's eight." I pulled up a picture of him on my phone and handed it across the coffee table for Mike to take.

He stared at the photo for a long time, his hand covering his mouth, his breath sounding ragged as it escaped from his nose. Finally, he handed the phone back and looked down. "I've sure missed a lot, haven't I?"

Spencer clapped his dad on the back. "It's okay. Right, Owen? You didn't know. It's no one's fault."

"I've never been proud of the way I lived my life back then," Mike said. "I'm not sure how much Spencer told you, but I didn't join the Marines because I wanted to serve my country or to make a better life for myself. It seemed like a better idea than jail. I'd be lying if I said that type of behavior with your mom was unusual or out of character for me back then. And I'm sorry for it."

Uncomfortable as I was with the topic, since it was my mom he'd had a one-night stand with, I was also highly interested in his story. "What changed for you?"

Mike looked at Spencer. "When I met my wife, everything changed. I tried to be better for her. I didn't always do a good job of it, though. And when she got sick, I can't say I made the best decisions. But, I tried."

"Spencer told me his mom passed away," I said, too afraid to mention Rebecca at that moment. My nerves were shot as it was. "I'm sorry for your loss."

He swallowed and looked at his hands. "Thanks. Anyway, I'm not perfect, but I've been trying to make it up to this guy, little by little. It's a tough pill to swallow, knowing how much more making-up I have to do with you now. And your son."

I didn't know what to say to that. I hadn't come here to make him feel guilty, though it didn't surprise me that he'd feel that way. Being a parent myself, I got it on some level. How would I feel if I'd missed out on Finn's whole life? I knew him and loved him, so the thought of that was unimaginable to me. But Mike hadn't even known I existed. Is he mourning time lost with me since he knows what it's like to be a dad?

Shaking my head, I resolved to move forward. I spent the next twenty minutes telling him everything I could about Finn. I showed him more photos on my phone and talked to him about our various activities as a family. Yeah, maybe we weren't big talkers in this family. But many parents could talk for hours about their kids. And grandparents? Well, if my mom was any indication, grandparents were even worse. And it made me feel all kinds of knotted up inside when I saw how interested Mike was in Finn's life. Spencer, too. It seemed like I'd hit the jackpot as far as long-lost relatives were concerned.

"I have to ask," Mike said, scratching his bald head, "did you and his mom split? I noticed she isn't in any of the more recent photos. It's okay if that's too personal, I know we just met."

"She passed away three years ago," I admitted, steeling myself for his reaction. "Hodgkin's lymphoma."

Wordlessly, he came over to my side of the couch and I stood, letting him pull me into a rough hug. By some miracle, I was able to hold it together and not completely give in to my emotions. I probably could have cried all over the guy's shoulder, but there was something about hugging a retired master sergeant that made me keep my cool.

"So, uh, did you two plan some kind of exit strategy for this meeting?" Mike asked after we broke apart.

Spencer chuckled and stood. "Everyone's over at West's apartment off base. Wanna come?"

"What's the occasion?" Mike asked.

"Fantasy draft."

Mike nodded once. "Let's do it."

4

RACHEL

To say that I was smitten the second I laid eyes on Spencer's long-lost brother was a total understatement. He walked through the door of Noah's apartment and it felt like all of the air left my lungs.

His traditional Marine haircut fit his square jaw perfectly, and he shared the same bright-blue eyes that Spencer and Mike both had. He was a hair taller than both of them, with broad shoulders and biceps that pulled at the fabric of his short-sleeved shirt. And when his gaze met mine, his full lips turned up slightly at the corners in a shy smile that somehow broke my heart and made it sing at the same time.

I shook my head to clear the fog and got off the couch to join the others in greeting this newcomer to the circle—even newer than me. Judging by the lack of a ring on his left hand, I hoped that meant he was also a *single* newcomer.

Noah West was the only single guy in the group, but there was something about him that didn't do it for me. He was handsome, sure. That was apparently a pre-req to hang with this crowd, but he wasn't my type. Besides, rumor had it he was in love with a movie star. She just didn't know it yet.

Spencer's brother, on the other hand, hadn't even spoken a word to me yet and I was already swooning. I shrugged internally. That was fine. He didn't need to speak. I would happily continue the pretend romance I'd already created between us in my head. That way it would never crash and burn when reality hit, like all of my past relationships.

It was my turn to meet him. I smiled brightly, holding out my hand. "Rachel."

"Owen," he said, shaking it firmly, which made me happy.

Most guys did this weird limp fish thing when they shook a woman's hand. It grossed me out every time. Why didn't they think we deserved to shake their whole hand?

"Nice to meet you," I said, reveling in the sparks between us as he held my hand maybe a second or two longer than necessary. Did he feel it, too?

"And you remember my pops, right, Rachel?" Spencer asked, pointing to Mike.

"Yes," I replied, waving at him. "Good to see you again, Mr. Hawkins."

"Mike," he insisted. "Good to see you, too. Now, we didn't miss the draft, did we?"

Our Host with the Most and this year's designated Fantasy League Commissioner rubbed his hands together. "No, sir," Noah said. "Let's get started."

The next three hours were spent laughing, bickering, trash talking, and eating chips and salsa like they were going out of style. Being a tomboy all my life, I was worried the rest of the girls in the group would separate themselves from the football stuff and gossip on the sidelines, but thankfully, they seemed just as interested as the rest of us were.

I wondered if these Marines had all found unicorn women who liked sports as much as they did or if they simply loved their husbands enough that they faked it to bond with them. Either way, I was all for it. In my perfect world, the couple who played together, stayed together.

After the draft, we all got up from our various spots in the living room and stretched our legs. Some went outside to enjoy the fresh air from Noah's balcony. Others went to the kitchen to grab more snacks and drinks. I couldn't help but notice Owen looking a little unsure of himself.

I sidled up next to him and bumped his arm with my shoulder. He was quite a bit taller than me and I looked up to meet his eyes. "Your team looks pretty good."

"Thanks," he replied. "Yours too."

"I'm glad you're here."

"Oh, yeah?"

"Now I'm not the new guy anymore." I grinned, hands on my hips.

Owen chuckled. "Did you recently move to San Diego or are you new to the group?"

"Both."

"And what do you think of San Diego so far?"

Bold by nature, I gave him a Cheshire smile. "It's getting better every day."

If I didn't know any better, I'd say the big, tough Marine in front of me was blushing. Note to self: this is a sweet one. He didn't latch onto my flirting with cheesy lines of his own. He simply *blushed*. Yep, I was a goner.

"So, I guess you already know how I fit into the picture, but how do you know these guys?" he asked, waving a hand to the general crowd.

"Long story short, one of my old roomies back in Texas married a guy who was in this group. And her brother was one of their friends, too. So, when I decided to move out to California and see what all of the fuss was about, she made sure I had a good group of friends to hang out with."

He turned his whole body toward me and stuffed his hands in his pockets. "That was nice of her. What's the verdict? Good group?"

"Very. Everyone has each other's back and it feels like more of a family than anything else. And speaking of family ... is Spencer your only brother?"

"Yep."

"I can't believe you found him with one of those DNA tests. I've heard of stuff like that on the news, though."

"Oh, yeah, it feels very reality-TV-like to me."

"Hey, who wants a boring life anyway?" I asked.

"Do you have a reality-TV-worthy story?"

I pursed my lips and looked at the ceiling. "Uh, well ... no. So I guess I have a boring life."

We both laughed at that, and the air seemed to crackle around us. I'd never been one of those girls who flirted by touching a guy's bicep or twirling her ponytail, but this guy made me want to do it. What in the world had been in the chips and salsa?

Noah walked up then, and I fought the urge to let my disappointment show. "Hey, man. So, you're air traffic control?"

"Yeah, you?"

"I'm a power liner," he replied. "But right now, I'm in QA."

"Yikes, bet that's fun," Owen replied.

They launched into shoptalk that went way over my head. I had no idea what QA was or why Owen sounded sarcastic when he referred to it as being fun. In the short time I'd been hanging out with this crowd, I knew Marines in a group couldn't go long without slipping into work mode and using way too many acronyms. I gave Owen my sweetest smile and excused myself to let them do their thing.

I walked onto the large balcony and took a seat in one of the patio chairs next to Ellie. "How's it going?"

"Hey, girl," Ellie said. "Pretty unbelievable about Spencer's brother, huh?"

I blew out a breath. "Completely."

"He seems really nice. Spencer won't shut up about how glad he is that Owen tracked him down."

"Aw, that's awesome. Just between us, I'm reminding myself to have some sort of chill around him," I admitted, keeping my voice low so no one overheard me. "I only talked to him for a minute, but I swear, as soon as he walked in the door, I was a goner."

Ellie threw her head back as laughter bubbled out of her. "Well, you'd be blind not to see the resemblance between him and my husband, so I guess I see what you'd like about him."

"Amen, sister."

"Did he seem into you?" she leaned in and asked, her voice hushed and her long blonde hair falling over her cheek.

"I mean, it's pretty clear he's got that shy thing going for him."

"And you are the opposite."

"So true," I allowed with a giggle. "But I don't know, *maybe*? It was a really quick conversation. And then Noah walked up and started talking about Marine stuff with him and I left."

Ellie rolled her eyes. "Men."

"I feel like I could ask him out, though. He didn't seem repelled by me or anything."

"I'm sure he wasn't," she scoffed.

I patted my thighs, decided. "Okay, wish me luck. I'm going in."

"Wait," Ellie said, holding up a hand. "Just so you know, he's got a—"

"Ellie?" Spencer poked his head outside. "Can you come unlock your iPad? Amelia wants to play that coloring game."

"We'll chat later," I said, hopping up so she could get her adorable goddaughter settled with her game. I crossed the balcony and slipped past Spencer into the house.

Owen was right where I'd left him with Noah, but

now Mike had joined them. I caught his eye, and my whole body warmed when he smiled at me. My confidence growing, I made a slight motion with my head, praying he'd come over here and not think I had a twitch or something.

He excused himself from the conversation and walked over to me. Butterflies took off in my belly, and the closer he got, the more on edge I felt. I hadn't reacted this strongly to any guy in as long as I could remember. Sure, I'd always been the kind of gal who asked the guy out first and didn't wait around for him to make his move, so that part was no different. I liked the rush. But the way he had my brain all frazzled and hoping I didn't trip and embarrass myself in front of him? Totally new territory.

"Hey," he said.

"Are you free this weekend?" I blurted, much less smoothly than I'd intended.

The corner of his mouth twitched. "What do you have in mind?"

I paused. *Shoot.* I hadn't actually taken the time to come up with something for us to do. I bit my lip. "Have you been to the beach yet?"

Owen shook his head. "Not yet."

"Maybe we can go for a run? If you're into that."

He flashed a quick grin, but I could see some deliberation in his blue eyes. He pulled his phone out, unlocked it, and went to the screen for a new contact before handing it to me. "Can I get your number? I have to see about some stuff before I can say for sure. But going for a run with you sounds great."

My mind swam with all of the things he could possibly need to "see about" before he could accept my invite. Was he even single? Or was he taken and he needed to juggle plans around with another woman before he could commit? Or what if he needed to end things with another woman before he could go out with me? Or was he actually just not that into me?

Ugh. I hated feeling self-conscious. It wasn't my style. I shook it off and tapped my info into his phone, then handed it back. "Hope to hear from you soon."

"You will. I promise."

5

OWEN

"He asked about me, huh?" Mom said, making a clicking sound with her mouth. "I don't even know how I feel about that."

"I didn't say much, don't worry."

"What *did* you say?" She started to bite at a finger-nail, a long-dormant habit, then realized what she was doing and crossed her arms tightly in front of her.

"I said you were the one who encouraged me to look him up."

"Did he ask if I wanted to see him?"

I raised a brow. "Do you want to see him?"

She fidgeted with the corner of her napkin then busied herself by stacking our empty dinner plates and moving them around the table. "I mean, no, what would we talk about anyway after all of this time? It would probably be awkward, right?"

"More awkward than me introducing myself as his son? At least he knows you exist."

She snorted. "I'm sure he barely remembered me."

"He seemed pretty clear." I studied her face, trying to figure out where this conversation was headed. "He said he'd seen you at the bar a few times, but that night was the first time he had the guts to talk to you."

She blushed but didn't reply.

My stomach knotted. Part of me hated the idea of her seeing him, I felt protective of her. This man had been with her and hadn't even suggested they exchange contact information. But then, he was also my father, and there was a childish wish buried in me that had always longed for them to find each other so we could all be a family.

I cleared my throat, hating the way this new discovery brought up so many old issues. "Mom?"

"Owen." She met my eyes and narrowed them like she used to when she was trying to figure out how to explain something to me. Then she sighed. "What else did you guys talk about?"

"Not much," I replied, trying to replay the conversation in my mind. "I told him about Finn."

"Ah, so it went well, I guess?"

I nodded. "Yeah, he reacted pretty good to the first

part about me, so it just came out that he had a grand-son, too."

"And how'd he take that?" She looked concerned, even more protective of Finn than she was of me.

"He was excited to hear about him. He asked a lot of questions, and I showed him pics on my phone. It was cool to see how into it he was. The idea of being a grandpa, that is."

She put her hand on her heart and made a crooning sound. "I'm glad. Ugh, just wait until he meets him. He'll be blown away, I'm sure. Finn's so smart. And sweet. And caring. I could just go on and on."

I laughed. "I know. If you guys do meet, I'm sure that'll be the only thing you talk about."

She got a faraway look then, almost like she was picturing that scenario.

"But," I said, "it got a little heavier when he asked about Rebecca ..."

"Oh, honey, I'm sure that wasn't easy to talk about."

"His wife died, too."

Her eyes bulged. "Really? I was going to ask if he was married to Spencer's mom. Was that her?"

"Yeah. Cancer. I didn't ask what kind. Spencer was twelve when it happened."

We sat in silence for a few moments while we processed the fact that I'd found my biological dad only to discover that I had the worst thing imaginable in common with him. Before we could continue our conversation, Finn came out from behind the kitchen island, his face somber.

Not surprised to find that he'd been hiding nearby, I held my arm out for him to step into. He buried his cheek in my shoulder and his small body melted against mine. I could feel his breath coming out in ragged bursts under my hand on his back. Finally, he pulled back and sat in the kitchen chair between me and his grandma.

"Sorry for listening," he said in a small voice.

I narrowed my eyes at him. "Are you?"

His mouth turned upward slightly. "Yeah."

"Why don't you go upstairs and brush your teeth and get ready for bed," I told him. "You've got school tomorrow."

"And PE," my mom said, wagging her eyebrows.

Finn glared at her. "*Grandma.*"

"What? I'm just saying."

I poked Finn's shoulder. "What's this about PE?"

"Nothing," he mumbled. "I like it I guess."

I shared a look with my mom and then looked back at Finn. "You *like* it? Since when?"

"Since he became friends with his new PE teacher. Right, Finn? What's her name again?" Mom asked.

"Mrs. Peters," he replied sourly.

"Bud, this is great," I exclaimed. "See, I told you it

could be fun. There are a lot of cool things you can do outdoors instead of playing on your electronics."

"To be fair, we've pretty much stayed in the gym all week so far. That's *indoors*, not out." He blinked at me, his mouth set in a hard line.

I let out a sigh. "Still. I'm a big fan of this Mrs. Peters for showing you how fun PE can be. You used to hate it more than spinach. Hey, I saw a flyer at the post office for baseball signups. Maybe we can check it out?"

Finn shot his grandma a look and got up from the table. "I'm gonna go brush my teeth."

"Mrs. Peters suggested that, too. She's going to be a coach." Mom snorted and then covered her face with her hand, trying to put on a serious face when he stuck his tongue out at her before running away. "Love you!"

"Yeah, yeah. Love you, too," he called from the stairs.

"He knew you were going to suggest baseball when you found out about PE," Mom said, grabbing our dinner plates and bringing them to the sink. "I'm glad your talk with Mike went well. My mind is still a mess over this whole thing. I can't believe you actually found him. All those years ... and then *boom*. You take one little test, and here he is."

I leaned back in my chair. "Not only that, but the fact that Spencer lives right down the street? It's too weird."

She pointed a soapy, gloved hand at me. "God's plan, sweetheart. Tell me more. What else happened?"

"We went over to Spencer's friend's house and had a fantasy football draft. His friends are cool."

"Do any of them have kids for Finn to play with?"

I shook my head. "No, the only kid is a little girl, and I think she's two? Or almost two, maybe? They're all a few years younger than me. But still cool. All married except for a couple of them. And ... well, there was one girl who was single."

"Oh?"

My mom was one of those moms who didn't like to pry, but she was so supportive that it made me want to tell her stuff anyway. It had always been like that and probably had a lot to do with the fact that it was just the two of us my whole life. Growing up, I didn't have two parents to bond with, I only had her. So she was kind of my person. And she didn't treat me like a kid. She talked to me like an adult. I tried to be the same way with Finn, too, because I think it did a lot for our relationship to have that way of communicating.

I rose from the table and stood across the kitchen island from where she washed the dishes. "Her name is Rachel. She just moved here from Texas. She invited me to go for a run with her at the beach this weekend."

Mom raised a brow. "And what did you say?"

"I got her number and told her I'd let her know."

She didn't say anything, merely pursed her lips and continued scrubbing the pot in the sink.

"What? Do you think I should have said no?"

"Do *you* think you should have said no?"

I scowled. "No."

"Okay, so no."

"Do you think I should have said yes?"

She stopped scrubbing and looked up at me. "Owen."

"Mom."

"You haven't dated anyone—"

I rolled my eyes and groaned.

"Honey, there's no right or wrong way to do this. If you're not ready, it's okay. She'll understand. And if she doesn't, she's not good enough for you anyway. It is the first time you've been asked out, though. So that's interesting. Since every other girl probably waited for you to ask her out. And since *that* wasn't going to happen ..."

Just thinking about Rachel had my nerves on edge. The way she'd confidently walked right up to me and introduced herself. My eyes had wandered over to her more times than I could count during the draft itself, and a couple of times she'd been looking back at me. More than once, I'd found myself grateful for the roomful of people because if they weren't there, I would have swept her into my arms and kissed her. And since I didn't know anything about her other than her first name, well, let's just say I didn't make a habit out of kissing people with so little information on them.

And all of that led to a heavy dose of guilt. My mom was right. I hadn't dated anyone since Rebecca passed. I hadn't wanted to. I hadn't even looked twice at another woman. So what was so special about the athletic brunette I'd met the day before?

"Owen," Mom said, turning off the water and tucking a strand of her dark-red hair behind her ear. "When I moved in with you—"

"Mom, don't." I didn't know what she was going to say, but I wasn't sure I was ready to hear it.

"Let me finish."

I waited a beat, steeling myself for what could potentially be a really emotional conversation. Though, I supposed it already was. Finally, I waved a hand for her to continue.

"When I moved in with you guys to help out when Rebecca got sick, I knew I was only moving in temporarily. I left my job at the hospital, promising to one day return before I was too old to walk those halls. But I thought it was because she was going to get better and you three wouldn't need me anymore. It broke my heart when she passed, and I stayed with you to help with Finn because I knew how much you both needed me. But that didn't make my position here any less temporary. Do you know what I'm saying?"

"Not really," I replied sullenly.

"I'm *saying*, I will stay with you and help you with Finn for as long as you *need* me," she continued. "I know you can't do your job without someone to care for your son. And I know he needs more than you can give him right now, but only because you can't be in two places at once. But someday, my prayer is that this will become a two-parent household again, and you won't need me here. I'll go back to work as a nurse and just be a grandma again."

My eyes traveled up to meet hers. "You can't move back to the East Coast unless we do. Whether you move out or not is beside the point. Finn can't lose you, too."

"Oh, sweetie," she said, sniffling. "Deal. I'm sure I can get a nursing job out here somewhere. And if you *never* get the guts to go on a date, I'll stay with you *forever*, busting your chops for not emptying your pockets before throwing your pants in the wash. And nagging you about whatever else I can until you go crazy and find a wife just to get rid of me."

I laughed. "Fine. I'll text her."

"Text who?" Finn asked.

Mom and I looked at each other, then I leveled my gaze on my son. "Mrs. Peters. I'm going to text her and thank her for inspiring you to like PE. And I'm gonna sign you up for baseball while I'm at it."

His face paled. "Don't you dare."

"I'm gonna," I threatened, pulling out my phone.

"You don't even have her number!"

I smirked. "I bet it's on the school's website. Should we look it up?"

"Dad, you better not!"

"Or what?" I roared, putting up my best tickling fingers and charging after him as he dashed away. "Why are you running? You can't escape The Tickle Monster!"

Finn heaved with laughter as I caught him on the couch and poked his ribs as he squirmed. "The. Tickle. Monster. Is. For. Little. Kids."

"You'll always be a little kid to me," I said, laughing.

Finn dashed out of my grasp and went to hide behind my mom, who patted his hair. "It's true, Finny. I still treat your dad like my little boy even though he's a grown-up and hates it."

Finn let out an exasperated sigh. "I'm doomed."

6

RACHEL

Finn ran up to me, sweat covering his brow. "I can't do this."

"Sure you can," I replied. "Have you ever played before?"

"Once."

I braced myself. "And how did it go?"

"I've got one word to describe how my last attempt at dodgeball went," Finn said, holding up a finger.

"What's that?"

"*Max.*"

I concealed a chuckle as he named his nemesis from his old school. I nodded. "Was Max a little too rough?"

"He threw the ball right at my nose. On *purpose.*"

I quickly surveyed the room to make sure everyone was doing what they were supposed to be doing while I chatted with Finn. "I'm sorry that happened. That is not the way to play fair. I know we haven't known each other for very long, but one of the mottos of my class is that if you can't play fair, you can't play at all."

"I know," he replied morosely. "I've heard you say it a few times."

"Good, then you know I run a tight ship around here. No one is going to throw a ball at your face on purpose in my class and get away with it. Okay?"

The rest of the class was starting to play, and Finn looked up at me with watery eyes. "Why do I need to take PE, anyway?"

My heart cracked. Finn was a sweet kid, and like any kid who didn't like PE, I wanted so badly to help him have fun in my class. But I understood that I couldn't make him love it just because I did or just because other kids did.

I bent to eye level and put a hand on his shoulder. "I know there are a million things you'd rather be doing right now."

"A trillion," he mumbled.

"Fine, a *trillion*," I allowed with a grin. "But if you don't take care of your body, where will you live?"

Despair morphed into anger on his little red face, and without another word, he ran away from me. I looked frantically at the rest of the class to make sure they were happily playing the game and then my eyes darted around to find Finn. He'd run to the far corner of the gym and crouched behind the bleachers.

I took off after him, jogging up to a fellow PE teacher at the other end of the basketball court with her third-grade class. "Hey, Susan, will you keep an eye on my bunch for a minute? I have a little situation with my newbie."

"Sure thing," she replied, her face sympathetic. She'd been teaching at the on-base elementary school for nearly twenty years, so she knew everything there was to know about transfer students having a rough transition. I made a mental note to talk to her about Finn later, in case she had any sage advice on how to make him feel more comfortable.

I made my way to where he sat, his shoulders shaking as he cried. "Finn?"

"Go away," he said, turning his back on me and tucking his knees up to his chest.

"Finn, I'm sorry, I can't do that. I want to make sure you're okay. I know I can't make you like PE, but I hope I can still make it tolerable for you." I reached a hand out to touch his shoulder, but then pulled it back. I didn't like to be touched when I was upset. Give me a hug when I'm on the verge of tears and they'll spill over for sure. "Is this about dodgeball? Or is it something else?"

He sniffed loudly, but didn't reply.

"Finn," I said in a warning tone, "when people are

upset around me, I tend to do really weird things to make them laugh. You don't want me to start quacking like a duck or jumping on one foot with my eyes closed, do you? Then you'll really need to run and hide."

I saw the side of his face shift as if he'd smiled and was trying to hide it. His shoulders quaked in a new way, like he might be stifling laughter instead of sobbing. My confidence grew.

"Okay, fine, I can take a hint. You don't want me to start acting silly. You want me to *sing*."

I made an exaggerated throat-clearing noise to let him know I was about to start, held my arm out like I had a microphone in hand, and opened my mouth to belt out the first thing that came to mind—Elsa's "Let it Go" from *Frozen*.

Finn spun around and waved his hands frantically in front of his wet face. "Okay, okay, stop, I'll talk to you."

"Thank you."

He tilted his head and searched my face. "Did they tell you about my mom? The school, I mean. I know they know because the lady in the office always gives me the sad eyes when she sees me. Drives me nuts."

Alarm bells went off in my head. This conversation was going to take a serious turn, and I had a feeling it didn't have anything to do with the bully he'd had in his last PE class. I shook my head. "No, they didn't tell me anything."

"She died three years ago."

A heavy silence hung in the air between us. I got down from my crouched position and sat on my butt, tucking my legs up to my chest like his. "I'm so sorry, Finn."

"Thanks. I didn't think you knew. You don't look at me like you feel bad for me." His face darkened. "Shoot, but you will *now*. Ugh. I shouldn't have told you."

"Finn, I *do* feel bad for you. That's a really sad thing and must have been really hard for you to go through. But now that I know, I promise I'll do my best not to give you the sad eyes."

He gave me a small smile. "Thanks."

"Thank you for telling me." I met his eyes, happy to see that there was a little bit of relief under all of his other emotions, almost like it felt good to tell me.

With a start, I replayed the conversation from before he'd run off. He'd gotten upset when I'd used the saying about taking care of your body. Maybe that meant his mom had died of an illness, rather than something sudden. Watching her get sick would make sense if he was triggered by the idea of not taking care of his body or being afraid of his body not being healthy.

Knowing how hard it must have been for him to tell me that she'd passed away, I figured it would be best not to ask him how she died. If and when he wanted to tell me, he would.

I peered through the bleachers at the other kids. "They really do look like they're having a lot of fun out there."

He followed my gaze, and I watched him as he watched them.

"Do you want to go join them? See if maybe you like dodgeball a little more since we're all going to play nice and fair?"

As I said the words, I realized that Finn's mom passing away when he was only about five years old was the epitome of unfairness. No wonder he was so fixated on other things in his life being as fair as possible. If my heart wasn't already broken for this kid, it was sure breaking now. The only silver lining was that I was a PE teacher. And one quality of any good PE teacher was the importance they placed on fair play. Even if it was only for fifty minutes a day, I vowed to make sure Finn felt safe from unfairness whenever he was with me.

L ater that night, just as I was losing hope about Owen accepting my invitation to go running, my phone buzzed on the counter. I craned my neck to read the screen, eyes growing wide when I saw the message preview. I quickly discarded the bowl I was washing and rinsed off my soapy hands, drying them just enough to be able to use my touch screen effectively. Swiping the preview open, I read, **Hey, it's Owen O'Malley. Sorry it's taken me so long to get back to you about this weekend. Are you still free?**

I couldn't help the grin that spread over my face as I typed out a quick reply.

Me: Still free, and still excited about it.

Owen: Great. I'm excited, too.

I wasn't ready to stop talking to him yet. I bit my lip, trying to decide how to extend the conversation. Finally, I figured I'd just do what I did best. I'd be myself and be blunt.

Me: Wanna keep chatting?

The sentence needed an emoji, of course, so I settled on the one with the heart eyes. If the guy didn't know I was interested, he was a blind fool. And if I seemed too eager for him, we wouldn't last long anyway. My mom always called me "high-spirited," and I knew it could be said with both a complimentary and a critical tone.

Owen: I'd love to. How was your day?

Me: It was a little rough actually.

Nervous to bring the mood down, I sent him a winky face and another message, before he could reply.

Me: It's improving by the minute, though.

Owen: You're smooth.

Me: Like buttuh.

I couldn't help the small giggle that escaped me as I slid down against the kitchen cabinet and sat on the floor of my kitchen. I could only afford a studio on my salary and I kept a clean place, so it wasn't like I had a ton of more glamorous seating options.

Owen: For real though, you can tell me about it if you want. We don't have to keep it light all the time. I can handle it.

I hesitated briefly. Well, we had to take the serious with the silly for it to be a real relationship someday, right? Might as well dive in.

Me: I found out some stuff about one of my students today that's not sitting well. I can't tell you details, but let's just say he's got a tragic past. And my heart hurts for him. I just want the time he spends with me to be a bright spot in his day, you know?

There was a long pause, and I worried I'd said too much. Finally, the dots showed up on my screen, indicating he was typing his response. I held my breath.

Owen: I can definitely see you being a bright spot in someone's day.

A satisfied smile made its way onto my face before I could stop it. Look at him, giving me a taste of the same flirting I'd dished out since we'd first met.

Me: Thanks. How was your day?

Owen: Kind of strange.

Me: Do tell.

Owen: So you already know that I'm Spencer's long-lost brother and that Mike is my dad.

Me: Yes. The three of you look so much alike.

Owen: Yeah, we do. Well, today my mom asked me for his info. She wants to reach out and meet up with him.

"No way," I said aloud, even though I knew he couldn't hear me. I shook my head and typed it out as my response, hopping up to grab my water bottle and taking my phone to my bed to finish chatting.

Owen: Yep. I gave it to her, but I don't know if she's called him yet. Not sure how I feel about it.

I didn't know anything about his family situation other than what I'd heard from the group. He showed up claiming to be Spencer's brother at Brooks's going away party, met Mike the day of the fantasy draft, moved here from the East Coast where Mike had apparently lived once upon a time. I figured I'd eventually get the rest of the story, but this little tidbit about his mom was even more juicy.

Me: Do you think your mom and Mike will spark some kind of romance? I mean, they clearly had a thing for each other at one point or you wouldn't be here.

Owen: Ugh, don't remind me!

Me: LOL

Owen: I guess I should chill out about it. They're both single adults, so if they like each other, good for them.

Me: That sounds very mature of you.

Owen: I'm a pretty mature guy.

I snorted. He was easy to talk to and had an interesting life. Ah, San Diego was definitely looking up.

Owen: I actually have some things I have to take care of. I'll see you at the beach on Sunday, though. What time and which beach?

I sent him a pin marking the location to meet me at Pacific Beach, the closest beach to my apartment. That way I could walk there and wouldn't have to worry about parking in the busy touristy area.

Me: Meet me here at eight?

Owen: Sounds great.

Me: Hey, that rhymed.

I sent him a silly faced emoji and he sent me the face with the sunglasses like he was calling himself Mr. Cool.

Owen: Good night, Rachel.

Me: Good night, Owen.

I flopped back against my pillows, phone pressed tightly against my chest. *Hurry up, Sunday.*

7

OWEN

"How do you think it's going so far?" Spencer asked. "I was a little nervous coming into it, but I think it's going really well."

I crossed my arms and turned from cleaning the grill to peer through the window. My mom and Mike were sitting at my kitchen island, Finn on the stool between them, smiling and laughing at whatever story he was telling them. They were the picture of the perfect grandparents, and I could tell my kid was eating it up.

It was the first time he'd ever had two grandparents give him so much attention at the same time. Rebecca's parents were divorced and both lived across the country from us, so he barely knew them. He would know them better if they weren't cowards who'd iced us out after her death, saying it was *too hard* to see how much he looked like her. It was the first thing they'd agreed on in all the time I'd known Rebecca, and it was the stupidest thing I'd ever heard. But that was their loss and a train of thought I didn't want tickets for.

I watched Finn with my mom and Mike for a moment. We'd just finished dinner. Our first dinner as a group. It was a completely normal, domesticated scene. A boy chatting with his grandparents over cookies and milk while his aunt did the dishes at the sink. His dad and uncle hanging out on the patio, cleaning the grill. The kind of stuff Saturday afternoons were made for.

I knew I should feel happy and full. I was glad I'd met Spencer and Mike. After all this time not knowing this half of my family, I was thrilled they'd turned out to be as cool as they were. But still, something was missing from this scene. Something I'd only just started thinking I might want to find again.

Big blue eyes and dark brown hair that was swept into a sporty ponytail flashed through my mind. And along with it, so did guilt. Was it okay? What would Finn say? Was this the part where he'd wonder if I was trying to replace his mom? Would he get mad? Would he hate anyone who came into our lives, no matter how cool and down to earth she was?

For the hundredth time that day, my chest tightened at the thought of going for a run with Rachel the next day. I could be making a colossal mistake letting a woman into this fold. If we—that is, both Finn and I—fell in love with her and she left us, I'm not sure if it would have been worth it. I'd always hated that saying about how it was better to have loved and lost than never have loved at all. Even three years after losing my wife, it made me angry.

Well, I wouldn't cancel on Rachel. It was too short of notice, and I went for a run every day, anyway. But I wouldn't take it further than that. And I definitely wasn't going to tell her about Finn.

"Earth to Owen," Spencer said, waving a hand in front of my face. "I *said*, how do you think it's going so far?"

I shook my head. "Sorry. Uh, I think it's going great. Finn really seems to like Mike."

"And I think he might not be the only one," Spencer said, wagging his eyebrows at me.

I recoiled. "Ugh. That's my mom."

"Easy, easy," Spencer said, holding his palms out. "I come in peace. Ellie whispered something to me about it, and I think she might be right. Look at them together. They seem kinda into each other."

I couldn't help the curl of my lip and the wrinkling of my nose. "She asked me for his number the other day. I'm pretty sure they've been talking. She's been acting weird ever since."

"Oh, yeah, I can totally see that. I bet that's why they're vibing so well together."

I made a noise that strongly resembled a harrumph.

"Come on, man," Spencer said. "Don't you want your mom to be happy? What if this was all meant to be? What if you getting stationed here was so we could all meet and *also* so they could get back together?"

"Spencer, they were never together. It was one night."

He waved a hand. "Man, whatever chemistry brought them together thirty-plus years ago is *clearly* still there. And they're both single. Why not?"

"We'll see," I said, gesturing at them with the grill brush. "Maybe they're just getting along for Finn's sake."

Spencer rolled his eyes so hard his whole head dropped backward. "Bro, you're delusional. Wanna bet I can get them together?"

"Oh, no you don't. Rebecca made me watch enough of those nineties chick flicks to know better than to make a bet about my mom's love life. I can picture that scenario blowing up in my face if she found out."

"Fine. You don't have to bet me. But you *do* have to get on board. Sometime I'll tell you about my grand plan that got my buddy Mills and his wife back together after they split. Worked like a charm. Trust me. This could be great."

I sighed. He was right. It *could* be great. Or it *could* be a complete disaster.

And judging by the determined look in his eyes, we were going to find out one way or another.

"I'm glad you could make it," Rachel said, pulling one toned arm across her chest to stretch it.

She wore tight floral running shorts with a neon-pink tank top, and the reflection of the color hit her cheeks in a way that gave her a flushed glow. Her brown hair was pulled into a ponytail again, and I wondered if it was her signature look. My gaze traveled from her hair, down the slope of her neck and over her shoulders, landing on the kind of biceps she likely spent a lot of time maintaining.

"Me too," I replied. "It's gorgeous out here."

She scanned the beach. "It really is. I love running in the sand. It's definitely not something I was able to do back home."

"Where in Texas is home? I didn't ask you the other day." I reached back to grab my foot as I pulled my leg up into a stretch.

"Fort Worth."

"Nice. I've never been."

She lowered into a lunge. "I wouldn't be from Texas

if I didn't say it's the best. Ten out of ten recommend a visit."

I chuckled. "Noted."

Thankfully, I caught myself before I said anything about how Finn had always wanted to go to Texas because he wanted to see a real-life cowboy. I'd only been with Rachel for a few minutes, and it was already proving hard not to talk about him when he was such a big part of my life. I couldn't exactly put my finger on my need to keep him from her. Maybe I wanted to protect him from getting hurt if this didn't work out. Better to feel her out when it's just me she's focused on. No need to factor in that I have a kid. Or that I'm a widower.

Dipping low into a lunge, I almost groaned out loud when I realized that was it. *That* was the reason I didn't want to tell her about Finn. If I told her about Finn, she'd likely ask about Finn's mom. And if she asked about Finn's mom, I'd have to tell her she'd passed away. And then the whole thing would be ruined because she'd look at me through that lens. Nope. Better to see if she liked me for me and not as some poor, pathetic, single-dad widower. I'd definitely gone through the darkness after Rebecca passed, but I didn't feel like that person anymore.

"You ready?"

Finished stretching, I nodded, holding my hand out. "After you."

We took off down the beach, falling into an easy rhythm, perfectly in sync. I didn't feel like I was holding back, and she didn't seem to be struggling to keep up. It was a nice pace. We jogged in comfortable silence for a few minutes. She didn't mindlessly chat to fill it, which I appreciated. I could tell she took exercising seriously, and I'd be lying if I said I hadn't worried this date would turn into more talking than actually running.

Rebecca and I had gotten together when we were pretty young, so I hadn't dated anyone other than her. Not as an adult, anyway. Teenager stuff didn't count. I hadn't given much thought to what kind of woman I'd like to date if and when I ever tried again, but as I took a glance to my right and noticed the way the sun reflected on the sheen of sweat on her skin, I thought maybe someone who liked to work out with me would be a good choice.

"So, I know you're a Marine," she said, only slightly out of breath from the difficult terrain, "but what exactly do you do with the Marines? Do you have the same job as Spencer?"

I shook my head. "Nope. I'm in air traffic control."

"Ooh, that sounds cool. And also, a lot of pressure, I bet."

"It was pretty intimidating at first, considering the

stakes, but it's all good now that I've been doing it for so long."

"And how long have you been doing it?"

I closed one eye and looked up, doing the math. "Almost eleven years now."

"Nice. So I guess you're doing the full twenty then?"

"For sure." I racked my brain for some other topic, since I'd been about to say something about how old Finn would be when I eventually retired. "What do you do?"

"I'm a teacher." Her breath was more ragged now with the conversation adding to the difficulty of running in sand.

Warning lights flashed in my head. That was definitely not a safe topic, considering I had a school-aged kid. I just wasn't ready to go there yet. "Right on. And how long ago did you move to San Diego?"

"Over the summer. Ugh, I seriously love it. I wish I'd had a reason to come out here sooner. I've never felt more at home somewhere. There's something about the beach and the sun and the vibe that makes me feel like anything is possible. You know?"

I hadn't stopped to think about it, but now that she mentioned it, there was something in the air here that gave me the feeling of a fresh start. I'd lived on the East Coast my entire life, and even though I'd hoped to get stationed on the West Coast years ago, it never happened. I'd gone to boot camp at Parris Island in South Carolina, my combat training and first duty station were both in North Carolina, and my second duty station sent me right back to South Carolina to Marine Corps Air Station Beaufort. The East Coast was definitely all I knew in my past, but the West Coast represented the future.

"Yeah," I replied. "I think I do."

"You probably get to travel a lot with the military. I haven't done much traveling, but I really want to."

I wrinkled my nose, my calves starting to burn from the effort of running in the thick sand. "I wish. Air traffic controllers don't stray far from the tower. I haven't even been deployed."

She balked. "Really? Isn't that a must for Marines?"

"For some jobs, yeah. But some ATC guys go their whole careers with only one or two deployments. I just haven't had mine yet."

I swallowed back any further explanation since part of the story involved me staying back from a deployment while my wife was sick. It was true that deployments were few and far between for air traffic control, but being a single dad made me pretty much non-deployable for a while there. My mom was set as the person responsible for Finn if I did ever leave for training or anything. The Marine Corps wouldn't send you somewhere if you didn't have adequate child care, thankfully.

"*Yet*, so does that mean you could deploy?"

I eyed her skeptically. "How detailed do you want me to be on this? Because I could give you the short answer or the long one depending on how much you care about the way it all works."

"I'm intrigued. Lay it on me."

"Okay, so basically, there are two sides to Marine Air Traffic."

"Okay."

"There's Station, which is what I am, and Detachment." The words came out a little choppy as my feet carried me through the sand. "Station does the tower and radar control that you've probably seen on TV and stuff. That's where every new controller starts. They earn their qualifications—or quals, as we call them—and then they can take those quals and move from Station to Detachment. That's where you'll start deploying."

"Cool."

"Then the more you deploy, the more expeditionary quals you earn. From there, you can then become a member or even a leader of a Mobile Marine Team, or MMT."

"Lots of acronyms and abbreviations in your world."

I chuckled. "Tons."

"And what does the MMT do on deployment without their tower? How do they control the air traffic ... mobile-*y*?"

I laughed at her made-up word. "They have some pretty cool mobile radar equipment. The teams get dropped in the middle of nowhere, set up a runway or landing zone, complete the mission, then pack up and disappear."

Her lips turned down and her brows lifted as she ran beside me. "Impressive. But you've never done that? You're not a new controller."

I proceeded cautiously. "Well, the MMTs are made up of only a handful of guys, four to six usually. The chances of deploying are low during peacetime with as many of us as there are. Besides, somebody has to stick around the tower to train new controllers."

She grinned. "Ah, so you're something of a teacher, too."

"Guess so." I almost asked her for more details about her job. What kind of teacher she was, what grade, what school she taught at. I wanted to know more about her. But potentially talking about kids and schools without admitting that I happened to have a school-aged kid of my own felt way too heavy on the lying-by-omission scale.

"Do you want to deploy?"

"Yeah, maybe someday. If I got to go somewhere

cool." And if I didn't think me leaving for half a year would destroy Finn.

Something caught my eye out in the ocean and stopped. She came up short, spraying sand as she dug in her heels. "What? What do you see?"

I squinted into the distance, shielding my eyes with the hand that held my water bottle and pointing out to sea with the other. "Look out there."

"Where?" She moved to my side, heat radiating off her body as she stood close and tried to see where I was looking.

"There," I said quickly, smiling when she gasped. "Did you see that?"

"Dolphins," she exclaimed. "Agh, I wish I hadn't forgotten my phone or I'd take a pic."

"You forgot your phone?"

"I live close-by. Plus, I have a smart watch."

"Still. That's not very safe."

She tore her gaze from the horizon and met mine. "I *feel* pretty safe."

We didn't say anything for a long moment, just looked at each other and breathed deeply from the exertion. Or maybe from the surprising connection between us that was so real and thick I could almost taste it. Her bright-blue eyes searched mine. I didn't know what she was searching for, but whatever it was, I wanted to give it to her.

She broke the spell she had over me by looking back out to the water. "I didn't know you could see dolphins from the shore. I thought you had to go on one of those fancy dolphin tours to see them."

I shrugged, angling my head down the beach and we took off running again. "I wouldn't know. But those dolphin tours look cool. It's on my list to do while I'm here for sure."

"How long are you stationed here?"

"Three years."

She nodded, and I wondered if it was weird to date someone who you knew had a limited time living in your city. Getting serious would mean potentially moving wherever they were sent at the end of the three years. I didn't know Rachel well—yet—but something told me she was adventurous enough to be okay with that. And smart enough to know she'd need to if she wanted to date an active duty Marine.

"What else is on your list?" she asked.

"Hmm," I thought about it. "I want to take a long drive up the coast at some point. Not on the freeways, but up Pacific Coast Highway. That road stays close to the water."

"That sounds nice."

"And I want to check out a Padres game in the spring," I went on. "It's too bad San Diego doesn't have a football team anymore."

"I can't *wait* for the first kickoff today. Maybe we could watch together? Go to one of those cool sports bars right on the beach?"

I wanted to say yes more than anything, but I already had plans to go to church with my mom and Finn. Then I figured I'd hang with him this afternoon and try to get him to put his book down long enough to watch the games with me. It hadn't really worked in all these years of trying, but maybe someday it would. I had a feeling the strategy of play calling and the running game versus passing game analysis would appeal to him once he was old enough to understand it.

"Ah," I said, genuinely wishing I could just invite her to hang with us, "I wish I could, but I already have plans."

She waved a hand. "It's totally fine. There are sixteen more Sundays in the regular season. Rain check?"

"Absolutely."

"Anyway, I know I said you had a good fantasy team, but mine's better." She said it with a wink, and my stomach flipped.

"Trash talking on our first date, huh?" I teased.

She narrowed her eyes at me. "Ooh, calling it a date and not a workout? Did I say this was a date?"

Alarm bells went off in my head. I was rusty. Out of

practice. But I swore this had date vibes all over it when she'd asked me.

I didn't have time to answer before she put an arm on my bicep and pushed me hard enough to almost knock me off balance in the sand. "I'm kidding. It's a date."

"Good," I said. And I meant it. I hadn't felt this light in a long time, and I was starting to become addicted to it.

We'd reached the end of the beach, large rocks blocking our path ahead. "Wanna take a water break?"

"Definitely."

We jogged up to the rocks and came to a stop. I took a long pull from the bottle I'd been running with, and my eyes traveled over to her as she did the same. She was flushed from the run, and I found myself itching to reach for the strand of hair that had come loose from her ponytail. Judging by the fact that she'd been the one to ask me on this date, I had a feeling she wouldn't mind.

The adrenaline from the workout coursed through me, making me brave. I lowered my water bottle and stepped over to her, our eyes locking. Running in the sand was a lot harder than flat ground, so we were both out of breath. She smiled and licked her lips, then caught her bottom lip between her teeth. With a steady hand—steadier than I expected—I reached out and grasped the chocolate-brown wisps between my fingers, smoothing them behind her ear.

My thumb traced a line over her ear and down her neck, my fingers sliding over the skin at the back of her neck. Her eyes never left mine as I pulled her slowly toward me, the hand that held my water bottle reaching behind her back and holding her close. If I thought too much about this, I wouldn't do it.

I brought my mouth to hers, and her entire body melted against me. Her arms circled around my neck as she raised up on her tiptoes. She tasted like salt, and the ocean air invaded my nostrils as I breathed her in. Our mouths moved together, perfectly in sync, just like we had been while on our run. I wasn't sure how long we stood there like that, wrapped in each other's arms, oblivious to the world around us. But when we finally pulled apart and I looked into her eyes, something told me my world would never be the same.

8

RACHEL

"So, what ever happened with your mom and Mike?" I asked, falling into step with him on our third beach run in as many days.

We both went for a run every day anyway, often before work, so it was easy to decide to do it together instead of apart. The sun was barely peeking over the horizon and the sand before us was still bluish in color. My favorite part was when the sun came up just enough for it to turn pink and then gold.

He paused before he answered. "I think they've been talking a lot. I'm not sure how I feel about it."

"What does Spencer think?"

"He's actively trying to get them together. He's a trip. I can see him doing a great job as the pesky younger brother if we'd grown up together. He's got just enough of it left in him as an adult."

I laughed, which made him smile down on me in the kind of way that made a blush creep up the sides of my neck. "I can see that. You're much more serious than he is."

"I'm not serious," he replied, giving me a mock glare.

"You're *super* serious," I said. "Or, I guess, thoughtful."

He pursed his lips. "I've been called worse."

"Anyway, I can totally see why Spencer would try to get them together. His mom died when he was a kid, right? He's probably so excited about his dad finding love again after all of that."

My heart squeezed as I thought about Finn from my third-grade class. That poor kid had the same story, and I just couldn't help but wish I could wrap him in a giant hug every time I saw him. I could see him wishing for the same thing as Spencer.

He cleared his throat. "So, um, what's your family like?"

"Oh, *psh,* remember how I said I don't have a reality-TV-like story?"

"Yep."

"I'm boring. My mom is also a teacher back in Texas. She's still married to my dad, who is a retired school bus driver. Now he just spends his time volunteering at all of the stadiums throughout the year."

"Volunteering how?"

"You know when you go to the game and there's the people who stand at the end of the rows checking tickets?"

He nodded. "Yeah, the ushers?"

"Yep. Living in Fort Worth has him close enough to all of the stadiums, so he's got year-round volunteering opportunities. Cowboys games in the fall, Mavericks games in the winter, and the Rangers in the spring."

"Living the dream for a sports fan," he said. "No wonder you're so into sports."

"Yes, I definitely get it from my pops."

"That's cool," he looked down at me and smiled that melt-y smile again.

We jogged down the beach in relaxed silence for a few moments. It was only an hour with him each morning, and most of it was spent controlling our breathing as we ran rather than talking, but I was starting to cherish it. I felt like I was growing close to him even in the silence we shared as we ran along the shore. And then in those heavenly moments where he'd steal a kiss or two, I felt like my heart was running away faster than my legs could keep up.

"Stop it," Ivy said, her face on the screen of my phone looking more like a teenage girl than the twenty-six-year-old she really was. "I can't believe he kissed you on the first date. A *daytime* date no less."

I sighed. "It was the right moment. We were both feeling it. Plus, we were all charged up from the run and everything."

"I also can't believe you're just now telling me about him and you've gone on three running dates now."

"I know, I'm sorry. But you know me, always getting my hopes up right before I crash and burn. I didn't want to tell you until I was sure he wasn't too good to be true. Though, I guess he still could be."

She frowned at me through the phone. "Don't get in your head. He sounds great. And I'm dying to see a picture. Send me one when you get a chance."

"He said he's not on social media, so I don't have one to send you. But I'll try to get him to take a selfie with me next time we hang out."

"Which is when?" my best friend asked.

"We're planning to keep up our morning run routine this week but he said something about a schedule change next week. And we're going to see a movie this weekend."

She wrinkled her nose. "I hate movie dates in the beginning."

"That's only because you talk too much," I teased.

Ivy threw her head back and laughed. "Whatever. That's cute, though. And lots of back-to-back dates."

I shrugged. "Yeah, kind of, but it's just a run. We'd both be doing it anyway so it feels casual enough."

"That's cool. Trust me, I get it. If I'd had the opportunity to go on a daily run with Jake in the beginning, I would have jumped on it. I literally wanted to spend every minute talking to him in the beginning."

"That's definitely how I feel. I have to stop myself from texting him throughout the day. It's bad."

Ivy chuckled, then shook her head. "I still can't believe the whole long-lost brother situation. *And* about his wife."

I'd been tipping back on the legs of my chair in the teacher's lounge, but when she said the word *wife* I had to catch myself before hitting the floor. "What?"

Ivy frowned. "What? You don't *know*?"

"Know what?"

"Girl, seriously? All of that time together and he didn't tell you? Owen has a son, and his wife died three years ago from some kind of cancer."

"How do you know?"

"Jake told me. He said he called Spencer and got all of the details as soon as he heard about them showing up at Spencer's house that day."

A son. A son whose mom passed away. From some kind of cancer. And they just moved here from the East

Coast. And I'd been there that day when Owen had shown up at Spencer's. When Ellie had gone to get Spencer to let him know someone was at the door for him, she *did* mention that he had a little boy with him. Ugh, I'd totally forgotten. The pieces of the puzzle slipped into place so easily that I couldn't believe my ears.

"Do you know what his son's name is?" I asked. "Is it Finn?"

Ivy shook her head. "I don't know, sorry. Who's Finn?"

"He's the sweetest kid in the world. I have him in my fourth-period class. He told me the other day that his mom passed away. Plus, he's a transfer student. How much you wanna bet that's him? It would be a pretty big coincidence if not."

"And you know I don't believe in coincidences."

I chuckled, letting out an exasperated sigh. "I can't believe this."

"I can't believe you didn't know."

"No one told me," I exclaimed.

She rolled her eyes. "Yeah, okay, but did you tell him you were a teacher?"

I nodded. "Yes, but we didn't go into detail or anything. And I didn't tell him I taught on base."

"Ooh, so he might not even know you're *Finn's* teacher."

"I'm sure he doesn't. I bet he wouldn't want to date me if he did."

"Are you mad he didn't tell you?" Ivy asked. "I mean, I can't imagine going through what he went through, losing his wife like that. I'm sure he had his reasons for keeping it to himself. At least in the beginning."

"I don't think I'm mad." I leaned forward on the lunch table and put my cheek in my hand. "I think I'm sad."

"Why?"

I looked at her like she had two heads, remembering with way too much clarity the embarrassment and shame I'd felt the last time a situation like this had gone south. "Because I'm not going to date my student's dad, Vee."

"Rachel, that was a long time ago. It probably wouldn't end up the same way."

"I don't care. That whole scenario was *not good* for my mental health. I made a vow right then and there that I'd never date a parent again, no matter how freaking handsome he was. And let me tell you, Owen is really, *really* freaking handsome."

"I need to see a pic."

I pursed my lips. "Well, since I'm probably not going out with him again, I can't help you there."

"I'm sorry, Rach."

"Me too."

All morning, I'd been super excited to spend my lunch break video chatting with my best friend and former roomie. But now that she'd dropped the bomb of all bombs on me, I wish I hadn't. Sure, it would have been nice to know ahead of time that Owen was Finn's dad, so I wouldn't have gotten my hopes up about him. But now that I knew, I wish I'd never found out. At least long enough to get one more run—and one more of those amazing kisses—out of the deal before I had to end things with him.

All of that being said, I didn't let it distract me from having an amazing PE class with Finn that afternoon in fourth period. He'd successfully played flag football for forty minutes, not once coming up to me to complain about unfairness or injustice. This was huge progress.

As I watched the grin spread over his face as his team scored a touchdown and they all celebrated together, I knew I was making the right decision in ending things with Owen. This kid needed more wins. He didn't need uncertainty and potential drama with his dad dating one of his teachers.

"Did you see that?" Finn asked, rushing up to me and wrapping his arms around my waist.

"I did," I said, returning his hug and stepping back to offer him a high five. "Great job out there today."

"Thanks. My dad would flip if I told him I played football. He makes me watch the games with him to get me to like it. But can I tell you a secret?"

I nodded, enjoying the image of sweet Owen trying to bond with Finn over football. "Tell me."

"I think *playing* it made me like it better than just watching it."

"Sometimes we need to learn something by doing it instead of just watching it. They call that *kinesthetic* learning."

A lover of big words and fun facts, he beamed. "Cool."

I bit my lip and crouched down to his level. "Hey, Finn, who's picking you up today? Grandma or Dad?"

"Dad."

Butterflies took off in my belly and it made me take in a sharp breath. "And, um ... what's your dad's name?"

"Owen."

Suspicions confirmed, I nodded. "Got it. I think I'd like to meet your dad today if that's okay with you. I'll meet you outside your homeroom after school and walk you out."

Alarm crossed his small features. "Why? Am I in trouble?"

"No, no, of course not. I want to say hi and tell him how good you're doing in PE. You're making awesome progress."

Finn shook his head. "No, thanks, Mrs. Peters. If you tell my dad how well I'm doing in PE, he'll for sure try to get me to play some kind of sport. Like baseball. My grandma told him about it and now he wants me to do it."

I grinned at him, catching the way he erroneously called me *Mrs.* Peters again. If he'd said that to his dad, no way he'd suspect that I was the one Finn was talking about. Did Owen even know my last name?

"Yeah, well, for what it's worth, I'd still love for you to consider joining the baseball team. I think it would be fun."

"Oh, man. Not you, too. Why can't you guys just let me play video games for the rest of my life?"

I rustled his hair. "Because we both care about you, little man. Now go on and get in line with the other kids. I'll see you after school."

The next two hours went by in a blur, and as promised, I met Finn outside his homeroom at the end of the day. "How was the rest of your day?"

"Good," he replied, falling into step with me toward the parent pick-up zone.

Nerves swam within me at the thought of not only seeing Owen again after spending the last three mornings running with him, but also seeing the look on his face when he saw me with Finn. A fleeting thought crossed my mind that upon seeing me, he might think I was some sort of deranged stalker who showed up at his kid's school. When we turned the corner and I saw him standing there in his cammies—and oh my, what a sight that was—and his neutral expression suddenly turned concerned, I thought I might be right. His expression softened, as he must have put two and two together about me being a teacher, and by the time we reached him, he had a smile for me.

"Hi," he said, then cleared his throat.

"Hey, Dad," Finn said, wrapping his arms around Owen's waist.

Owen rubbed Finn's back, eyeing the Department of Defense employee badge on the lanyard around my neck. "Who's your friend, bud?"

I smiled widely and stuck out my hand for him to shake as Finn said, "This is Mrs. Peters, my PE teacher."

"Mrs. Peters?" he asked, raising a brow as he shook my hand.

"*Ms.* Peters," I corrected.

"Ah-ha."

We both worked to stifle our laughter as the ridiculousness of the situation sank in. He held my hand between us, still shaking it up and down, still staring into my eyes in a way that made me want to jump into his arms.

I was barely aware of Finn standing between us. His little head whipped back and forth, looking at each of our faces. We only had eyes for each other, so Finn swept his arm up and waved a hand between us, breaking the spell.

"What, Finn?" Owen asked, turning his attention to his son.

"Why do you look so weird?" he asked.

"I don't look weird," Owen replied, then flashed me a smile. "Sorry. I didn't—"

"I know. Neither did I." I finished for him. "But um ..."

Owen's brow furrowed. He reached into his pocket and pulled out his wallet, then took out a few dollar bills and handed them to Finn. "Hey, bud, can you go right there to that vending machine and get us a couple of Gatorades?"

Finn's eyes lit up. "Yeah, thanks!"

We watched him run away for a moment, then turned back to each other when he'd made it across the grassy area to wait his turn in line for the machine.

"You're the famous PE teacher inspiring Finn to like sports?" Owen asked.

I nodded. "Guilty."

"I had no idea."

"Well, it probably doesn't help that he keeps calling me Mrs. Peters."

He pointed a finger at me. "I definitely didn't picture you when he called you that. I pictured the stereotypical, middle-aged gym teacher from the movies."

"That's my coworker."

"Noted."

I turned to check on Finn. He was still waiting for his turn at the vending machine. He looked over and caught my eye, giving me a thumbs up. I returned the gesture, then turned back to Owen. "I really like Finn."

"I'm glad." His smile was big. Proud. Warm.

Trying to ignore the fact that I liked him even more when attaching him to Finn, I crossed my arms over my chest. "But I can't date my student's dad."

His eyes tightened around the edges, the shade his camouflage hat provided made them look even deeper blue. "You can't? As in, it's some kind of rule with the DOD school district?"

"I don't think it's an official rule, no. Definitely frowned upon, but not a hard-and-fast rule."

He glanced back at Finn, and I turned to look as well. He was just stepping up to the machine. Owen turned back to me. "But it's a hard-and-fast rule for *you*?"

"Yes," I confirmed.

He took a step forward, lowering his voice. "Are you sure?"

He smelled like the ocean and warm spice, and I was instantly transported back to the beach and the feeling of his strong arms wrapped around me. The way his hand had grazed the back of my neck and then pulled me in to kiss him. The softness of his lips. Lips that were now, much, *much* too close for comfort. I took a step back, needing the distance to keep my resolve.

Just in time to save me from changing my mind, Finn came running back up to us. He held three Gatorades in his small arms. "I got one red, one blue, and one purple. Which one do you want, Mrs. Peters?"

I chuckled as Owen's eyes met mine, a rueful smile on his lips at the misuse of my name again. "Blue, please."

Finn happily handed me the blue one, then handed the red one to his dad. "She asked for the blue one first, so you can have the red one. Sorry, Dad."

His mouth twitched. "It's okay. Thanks, bud."

"Is blue your favorite?" I asked him.

He nodded.

I held it out. "Wanna trade?"

"No chance. Enjoy." He cracked open the red one and took a gulp.

Finn's eyes were wide when he looked at me. "He must really like you. He loves the blue one."

"All right, bud," Owen said, putting a hand on Finn's shoulder. "Let's let Ms. Peters get on with her day. It was nice to meet you."

Knots formed in my belly at his formal tone, like we hadn't shared one of several amazing kisses on the beach earlier that morning. "You too."

9

OWEN

"You're finished with your snack? Okay, go upstairs and do your homework," I said, pointing up the stairs from my seat on the couch.

His shoulders sagged. "Already?"

"You've been home and relaxing for an hour, Finn. You need to get it done before dinner."

He opened his mouth to protest, but one warning look from me was all it took to get him out of his chair and heading for the stairs.

"Hey," I called after him, and he turned. "Forgetting something?"

He looked confused at first, then the light bulb went on, and he ran back to his place at the table. He gathered up the trash from his snack of string cheese, crackers, and grapes off the vine, and threw them in the trash. Then he headed for the stairs to do what I'd asked.

I sighed and sank deeper into the couch, my eyes on the TV but my brain at the beach with a certain gorgeous brunette. Finn's teacher? What were the odds? There were a lot of things going on in my life that my mom kept referring to as divine intervention, in a good way. But this? Not good. Not good at all.

Speaking of, my mom walked through the garage door, grocery bags lining her arms. I tossed the remote on the cushion next to me and hopped up. "Hey, is there more?"

She heaved the bags onto the counter and pulled her arms out of the looped handles. "Yep. Full trunk."

We headed to the garage, loading our arms up with more groceries. Peeking into the bags, I was reminded yet again how nice it was to have her there to help. She'd truly picked up the slack when Rebecca had gotten really sick and I hadn't had the time or energy to do everything myself. Then afterward, having her stay and make sure Finn had the love and attention he deserved meant the world to me. Deep down I knew it wouldn't be forever, but while she was there, I was immensely grateful for the two-parent household vibe.

"How was your day?" she asked, studying my face.

Busted, I gave her a sideways smile. "Started great, then it took a turn."

"Uh-oh. Trouble in paradise?"

She knew about my running dates with Rachel since she was on Finn duty while I was gone. "You could say that. When I went to pick up Finn from school today, I found out *Rachel* is actually the amazing *Mrs. Peters* Finn is always talking about."

My mom stopped abruptly in the doorway to the kitchen, both of us holding mounds of groceries. "She's married? That little—"

"No," I interrupted, nodding toward the kitchen, "scoot, this is heavy."

She snorted and continued to the kitchen. We began putting away the food as I explained. "He keeps saying *Mrs.* Peters, but it's actually *Ms.* Peters. She's not married, but she is his PE teacher."

"Ah, I see. Well, for what it's worth, I met her. She's *beautiful.*"

I sighed. "I agree. But she doesn't want to date her student's dad. So, it's over."

Mom had been putting a box of mac 'n' cheese in the cupboard when she stopped, holding the box in the air. "What? That's ridiculous. Does she know what year it is? Who cares?"

"She does, I guess. I have to respect it."

"I'm sorry, honey. I know how hard it was for you to

get back out there. But don't fret. Think of this as a prac-tice run. No pun intended."

I snorted at her dumb joke. "Right."

"I'm serious. Now when you find the right woman, you'll have already gotten a little practice dating again. It won't be as scary next time."

I nodded. "Yeah, maybe. I'm not sure if I want to deal with that any time soon. I mean, she's the one who asked *me* out. I wasn't exactly looking for this when I showed up at that fantasy football draft. And now here I am crashing and burning right at the beginning. Doesn't seem worth it."

Her eyes watered a little but she waved a hand in front of her face and went back to unpacking the grocery bags. "Sorry, don't mind me. You're my baby, that's all. I want to see you happy."

"I know, Mom."

She held the extra-large bag of finely shredded Mexican cheese against her chest and sighed. "You really liked her, didn't you?"

I didn't want to believe it was true after only a few runs on the beach, but I really had liked her. Logically, that was weird since we barely knew each other. We'd only shared a few fantastic kisses and had a few great conversations. It wasn't much to go on. But when I'd first caught her eye at the football draft, something inside me had lit up. Some-thing long dark and dormant had come back to life. It was almost like my heart recognized hers as something ... familiar. Something meant for me. Every time I thought about it like that, I felt dumb and dramatic, but it was true.

I shook my head. "Doesn't matter now, does it?"

Mom put her hands on her hips. "Owen O'Malley, I did *not* raise you to give up so easily. If you care about this girl, you need to go after her. Suggest that you keep it up with this running habit of yours. Even if it's just as workout buddies. The beach is a very romantic place. Maybe she'll come around."

Laughing, I shut the door to the pantry. "Mom, it's kind of a thing to respect a girl when she says she's not into you."

"Did she say she wasn't into you, or did she say she didn't want to date her student's dad?"

She had me there. I let my silence speak for me as I blinked at her.

"Exactly," she replied.

Movement caught my eye at the end of the kitchen island. I scowled. "Finn Patrick O'Malley. Stand up."

A scruff of chocolate-brown hair and a pair of deep-brown eyes—Rebecca's eyes—raised up at the edge of the island. "Hi."

"Hi." My tone was icy. "How much of that did you hear?"

"Not much."

I sighed. "Did you get your homework done?"

The brown hair shook as he nodded, his lips still not visible from beneath the counter. "Yep."

"Go wash up for dinner, then."

He took off for the stairs, and I looked at my mom. She was standing there with her hand over her mouth, stifling a laugh. "Well, now. I guess we'll find out soon how much he really heard."

After dinner, I'd just flopped onto the couch to watch TV when Finn's voice came from upstairs in his familiar call. "I'm all done!"

"Be right there," I replied, heading up the stairs.

I entered his room just as he was climbing into his loft bed and pulling his Minecraft comforter up to his chin. As was our habit after he brushed his teeth and got in bed, I walked up to the edge of the bed and arranged his various stuffed animals alongside him. They had to be in a specific order: Mario, Spider-Man, Pikachu, Gray Matter, and finally, Leonardo the Ninja Turtle.

Finn was lost without his routines, a fact that my mom thinks he'll grow out of. I wasn't so sure. He'd probably always be comforted by things that made sense and could easily be controlled. After what we'd gone through, I didn't blame him.

"All set?" I asked, finished with the routine.

"All set."

I patted his leg once and turned to leave. "Good night, buddy. Love you."

"Wait."

"Yeah?"

"Do you think you'll get married again?"

I swallowed. "I don't know. Why?"

"Just wondering."

"Do you want me to? That's not really something we've ever talked about."

He nodded. "Grandma says you're never too old to find love again."

I raised a brow. "Oh, did she?"

"Mm-hmm. I think she's finding love with Grandpa."

The bark of laughter that escaped me had to be quickly covered up by a coughing fit when I saw him furrow his little brow at me. "Sorry."

"Is that bad?" he asked.

"It's not bad. How do you know that, though?"

He bit his lip but didn't answer.

"Finn. Tell me."

"I heard her talking on the phone with him," he admitted, keeping his eyes closed as he said it.

"You eavesdropped on a private conversation between Grandma and Mike?"

"*Grandpa*," he corrected me.

"Grandpa," I allowed, the word feeling foreign on my tongue. "Seriously, Finn, the eavesdropping has got to stop. It's disrespectful."

"But you always call me a special agent."

My shoulders softened and I rested my arm on the side of his loft bed. "Yes, I know, bud. It was cuter when you were younger, but you're getting older and you're starting to understand adult conversations that aren't meant for you. Do you know what I'm trying to say?"

"Well, yes, but if I'm getting older, then it should be more okay for me to hear adult conversations."

I shook my head. "No, that's not what I meant."

"Don't you wanna know what she said to him?"

Yes, I did. I knew I shouldn't, but I really did. "No, bud. It's none of my business."

He sat up. "*Okay*, but she sounded really happy. She was all giggly and stuff."

I laughed at his grossed-out expression, but then my own face probably matched his as I thought about my mom flirting with someone. "All right, seriously. I don't want to hear about their conversation, and you need to stop listening to conversations that aren't meant for you. Got it?"

He nodded with a pout on his full lips. "Okay. But I did hear her say she'd move out if you got married."

This made my brows shoot up. "Did she?"

"Yep. Which is why I asked if you were gonna get married. Do you think she'll move in with Grandpa?"

"Okay, that's enough. Go to sleep, Finn." I patted his leg one last time and headed for the light switch, flicking it out as I left the room.

"You could marry Mrs. Peters."

His small voice carried into the hallway, causing me to stop dead in my tracks. Clearly, he'd heard most of my conversation with my mom about Rachel earlier. I could go in there and acknowledge it, or I could just keep walking and pretend I didn't hear him.

The only problem was, I did hear him. And when he'd asked me if I was going to get married again, she'd been the first thing that popped into my mind. Rachel would probably fit in with us perfectly. It was easy to see, even with as little as I knew about her. Too bad she'd already ended things before we could get far enough to find out.

I knew it wasn't a good idea, but I pulled my phone out of my pocket and sent her a text.

Me: I know you said you wouldn't date a student's dad, but is there any harm in just being running buddies?

I leaned against the wall in the dark hallway and

awaited her reply, my breath catching when I saw the dots appear to signal she was typing.

Rachel: I know what it's like to kiss you, Owen O'Malley. We can't just be friends.

My stomach tightened at the thought of having her in my arms, sweaty from our runs and yet still smelling fresh like the sea. I'd never simultaneously had my hopes crushed and my ego boosted at the same time. I had no idea what to say. Maybe there wasn't anything I *could* say. With a heavy sigh, I slipped my phone in my pocket and headed for bed.

I pulled into the school the next day to pick up Finn, wondering if I'd see Rachel again. I only had a few more opportunities to torture myself with seeing her this week before I switched from my week on day crew to my week on night crew. When I was on night crew, it would be my mom who picked up Finn while I was just starting my workday.

When Finn ran up to me alone, I bit back the urge to ask about his PE teacher and decided to be more general. "How was your day?"

"Fine," he replied, waving a hand. "Can we go to the Exchange? Right now."

"Why?"

"I need to get something."

I scratched my head. "What could you possibly have to get at the store? You're eight."

"You know how they always have local artists set up outside? My friend's dad is going to be there selling his paintings of the beach and I want to get one for my room."

"Really?"

He shrugged. "Yeah, I like the beach."

"I haven't even taken you yet."

His eyes narrowed. "Dad. I'm trying to support my friend. And I live in San Diego, where there's a beach. Can you just take me?"

"How much are these paintings?" Dollar signs flashed in my mind as I thought about how much an artist might charge for original paintings. I wasn't an expert or anything, but painting a beach seemed like the kind of hard work you could charge a mint for.

"I have no idea. Can we go find out?"

I looked at my watch. "Fine. But if I say they're too much, don't argue with me in front of the guy. It'll be really awkward."

"Deal." We walked to the car and headed over to the department store on base. He got out and was practically skipping up to the entrance. I saw the big, black racks in front of the doors that held paintings of various shapes and sizes. When we got close enough that I could see the people milling about, my heart picked up speed. Among the smattering of people gazing at the paintings on display was Rachel.

She looked up as we approached, and her surprised look quickly turned into a warm smile when she met my eyes. Much too soon, she turned the smile on Finn as he ran to hug her tightly around her small waist. "Hey, Finn. You didn't tell me you were going to come check out these paintings after school, too."

Finn looked nervously at me. "I want one for my room. I can't believe you beat us here."

"I have a prep period at the end of the day. I can see why you'd want one for your room. They're beautiful." Rachel's eyes traveled over the artwork and she beamed. "Want to help me pick one out for my room?"

He nodded. "Yes! I'll go look over there."

We watched as he left us to go look at the tower of paintings in the far corner of the outdoor gallery. Then Rachel turned her blue eyes on me, and my whole body warmed. "Hi."

"Hi," I replied.

"Finn told me his friend's dad was the artist and that I *had* to come check out these paintings," she explained. "You know, since he knows how much I love the beach."

I snorted. "He told me I had to bring him here so he could get one for his room. Kid's never even been to the beach. I should have known something was up."

She tilted her head at Finn with a wry smile on her lips. "Do you think he knows about us?"

"Oh, I know he knows. He has a serious eavesdropping problem."

"Really? Does that mean you were talking about me?" She pulled a strand of her long hair from her ponytail and played with it between her fingers.

"I was."

She quirked a brow. "And what were you saying?"

I pursed my lips, unsure if I should be honest or make something up. I settled on honesty. What did I have to lose? "I was saying I was bummed you didn't want to date your student's dad."

She blushed. "I see."

"Seems like he might be trying to make it happen anyway."

"He's going to wind up disappointed if that's his plan, Owen." All of the flirtatiousness vanished from her eyes. "I'm serious."

"Okay." I swallowed, tearing my eyes from hers and looking at the painting behind her head. It looked remarkably like our beach. "You should get that one."

She turned to look at it, then nodded, taking it off the rack. "You're right. It's perfect."

She gave me a small smile, and for the first time, I saw a familiar sadness appear in her eyes when they met mine. "Full disclosure, I know your wife passed away. Finn was having a rough day recently and he told me. It was before I knew you were his dad. That's *how* I found out, actually. The dots connected pretty quickly once I heard from the girls that your wife had passed away. I'm so sorry for your loss."

"Thank you."

"Did you find one you like?" Finn asked, running up to us.

She showed him the painting. "Yep. What do you think?"

"I love it," he replied.

"Me too," I agreed.

"Man, I really want to go to the beach." He gave his best pout, complete with a heavy sigh and hanging his little head.

I snorted, but Rachel looked up at me with sympathetic eyes. "Maybe we could take him there to get some ice cream? As friends, of course."

My heart felt like it actually may have skipped a beat. But I played it cool with a shrug. "Yeah, I don't know. Finn, would you want to do that?"

"Yes," he exclaimed, his eyes lighting up. "Yes, please!"

"I'm not sure about the ice cream though. Don't want you to ruin your dinner," I said.

Finn wrinkled his nose. "Oh, come on, Dad. Don't be a downer."

"Yeah, Dad," Rachel teased. "Don't be a downer. We need ice cream. Right, Finn?"

I looked between the two of them, surprised at the turn of events but happy about it. I wasn't one to look a gift horse in the mouth. If Rachel wanted to go to the beach with me and Finn, even if it was just as friends, I was all for it.

"All right, let's go." I hooked my thumb at my car behind me. "But we'll meet you there. I have to run home and change first. Can't leave base in cammies."

And if I wasn't mistaken, I thought I saw a little bit of disappointment in Rachel's eyes.

10

RACHEL

An hour later, we'd finished our ice cream and were letting Finn run in the surf with some boys his age while we leaned against the sea wall and watched. He was under strict instructions not to go more than knee-deep into the ocean, but I still couldn't help but watch him like a hawk in case he got swept out to sea or something. I took comfort in the fact that there were lifeguards nearby.

"This is nice," Owen said, bumping me with the side of his arm. "Thanks for the invite."

"I couldn't resist seeing Finn's first time at the beach." I eyed him. "Even if it does mean spending more time with you and not being able to kiss you anytime I want."

"*Sweet Home Alabama,*" he said, pointing at me.

I narrowed my eyes at him. "Yes. Didn't peg you for a chick flick guy."

"Rebecca forced them on me. Every night was movie night for a while there."

I couldn't fight the rock that settled deep within me. "That's sweet."

"Mm-hmm."

"How long was she actually sick?"

"About two years." His gaze was unfocused as he watched his son frolic in the water.

I pictured him as the doting husband, taking care of his sick wife and cozying up on the couch with her to watch chick flicks. I had no idea what she looked like, of course, but I figured she must have had beautiful dark hair and chocolate-brown eyes, like Finn.

A thought occurred to me then. "Hey, your mom didn't pass on her red hair to anyone. You're blond with blue eyes, like your dad and Spencer, and Finn has dark hair and eyes. Like Rebecca, right?"

He chuckled, crossing his arms. "Yeah, Rebecca was Italian. But, just between us, my mom's red hair isn't real."

I gasped. "She dyes her hair?"

"Yep. I mean, I think it's still like a strawberry-blonde color when it's not that dark red color, but I wouldn't know. She's been dyeing it like that since before I was born."

"I'm shook. I mean, I knew she was the Irish one, so I really bought it."

He winked. "I think that's what she's counting on."

"So, um, how is Finn doing with everything? The move, I mean. When we first met, we talked a little bit about how scary it was to move to a new place. I told him I knew how he felt, being new here, too."

"Were you scared when you first moved here?" he asked.

"I mean, kind of? I've never lived outside of Fort Worth. And I've never lived alone. I went straight from my parents' house to my college dorm to sharing a place with two fellow teachers. Now I have a tiny studio by myself. It's a little too quiet sometimes, if I'm being honest."

He pursed his lips. "Hmm. I've never thought about it, but I've never lived alone either. Mom's house, boot camp, barracks, then got married and had Finn."

We watched him together in silence for a few minutes, then Owen cleared his throat, making me look over at him. He was looking back at me, studying my face, seeming like he wanted to say something but not sure if he should.

Being as bold as I was, I wanted desperately to say what we were both probably thinking. This was dumb and we should just be together. We had the chemistry. We had the opportunity. And we even had the potential for a future, since now that I was in the DOD system, I could probably get a job at another base school whenever he had to move.

But thinking ahead like that and jumping headfirst into a relationship was how I always wound up heartbroken later. This man and his adorable son had the power to crush me, and I just wasn't ready to let it happen.

In all of my thinking to myself, I hadn't noticed just how close Owen's face had been getting to mine.

"He seems to be adjusting really well," I said, determined to break the moment.

Owen leaned back and returned his gaze to Finn. "Yep, he's doing great. I know your class helps a lot."

"Good, I'm glad."

His jaw clenched and he checked his watch. "We should get going. He's probably got homework."

"Oh, yeah, totally. I understand."

He called to Finn, who waved goodbye to his playmates and came running.

"We'll walk you to your car," Owen said, gesturing to the parking lot.

I shook my head. "I live right up there. I parked at home and walked over since you had to stop at home first."

Finn's brows shot up to his forehead. "You live close enough to the beach that you can walk?"

"Yep."

"Oh, man. If I were you, I'd never leave the beach. It's so much fun."

I knelt down and ran a hand over his sandy hair, wet from being splashed. "If I didn't have to work so hard to afford to live here, I wouldn't. The sea makes everything better, don't you think?"

He nodded, a wide smile on his flushed face. "Yeah. Everything."

"Y ou need to level with us," Ellie said, taking a sip from her wine glass, "what happened the last time you dated a student's dad?"

I covered my face with my hands. "Ugh. Do I really have to?"

"Yep."

"Sure do."

I looked up at Ellie and Olivia. The three of us sat around the fire pit at Spencer and Ellie's house. With wine glasses in hand and fixin's for s'mores within arm's reach, my two newest friends were ready to hear all about the mess that was my love life. I'd already filled them in on our amazing running dates, the kisses I couldn't seem to get out of my head, Finn, and the breakup.

"Okay." I took a deep breath and a sip from my wine glass. "The last time I dated a student's dad was a few years ago. We met at Open House at the beginning of the school year."

Ellie held up a hand. "Wait. Is this story rated PG?"

I picked up a marshmallow from the bowl in my lap and chucked it across the fire at her. "Hush. Of course it is."

She snatched the marshmallow from where it landed on the wicker couch next to her and popped it into her mouth. "Just checking."

"*Anyway*, so we met at Open House. It was the beginning of the school year, and his daughter was seriously the cutest thing. She had on this twirly dress and a huge bow in her hair, which is so opposite of me in every way. When I was little, I only wore shorts and was always scraped up from climbing trees and jumping off of the playground structures."

The girls laughed, Ellie saying she was the same way and Olivia identifying more with the girly girl.

"The dad—Andrew—hit on me right away. He was super forward, and at first, I thought that meant he was a strong, confident guy. Which I like. Or at least, I used to. But I learned pretty quickly why he'd gotten divorced. He wound up being very controlling and manipulative."

Ellie cringed. "Uh-oh."

"And the weirdest part was, so was his ex. He must have told her we were dating just to make her mad. They were a few years older than me and I think he played it off like I was the younger model he traded her in for, you know?"

"Yuck," Olivia said, her lip curling. "What a jerk."

"Yep. So the ex-wife made my life miserable with the school because she kept filing complaints about the fact that we were dating. She said it made her uncomfortable, and the administration was constantly on my back about it. Then, when she realized they weren't going to fire me over it because it didn't violate any school policies, she started spreading rumors to the other parents about me."

"That sounds awful." Olivia took a sip of her wine and shook her head. "How did it end?"

"Well, it wasn't a quick thing. I was wrapped up in this mess for about a year. Like I said, he was really controlling. I couldn't seem to make a clean break. Plus, to be honest, I fell in love with his little girl. Her name was Bella, and for a short time, she really started to think of me as a second mom. Finally, his job took him to another state and he wound up getting back with his ex, anyway. I was devastated. Not so much because of him but because of Bella."

"Oh, goodness," Ellie said.

Olivia sighed. "It really does sound awful. But, as

bad as it sounds—and trust me, I would *not* want to deal with that—I fail to see what it has to do with Owen. I mean, not to sound cruel, but he doesn't have a wicked ex-wife to deal with, you know?"

A loaded silence hung over us as we thought about it, but then I sighed. "I guess it's not so much that I'm worried about the ex-wife, as it is the effect all of it had on that sweet little girl. It was really sad watching her stuck in the middle of all of that drama. Not only was she dealing with her parents' rocky divorce, but she also had to deal with her dad dating her teacher, and all the other kids started picking on her for it. The whole thing got out of hand really quickly, and before I even knew what was happening, it was this tangled web of chaos with sweet little Bella stuck right in the middle."

Their faces softened, and Olivia reached over and patted my knee from the seat next to me. "You're a good person for worrying about Finn like that. We all met up at the playground the other day and Amelia is obsessed with him. And he's so sweet with her."

"See?" I threw up my hand with a groan. "The whole friend group is so interconnected. If we dated and it went bad, that would cause so much drama for Finn outside of school, too. I love you guys. I wouldn't want to get booted from the group if we made a go of it and then broke up. There are *always* sides in these kinds of things."

Olivia and Ellie looked at each other knowingly, and Ellie sighed. "We experienced that while Matt and Olivia were split up for about six months. No one got booted out, but we didn't hang as a group the entire time."

"Exactly," I said.

"Rach," Olivia said, holding up a finger, "there's something else that could happen if you guys give it a go."

"What?" I asked, bracing myself for more bad angles I hadn't considered yet.

"You could wind up happily together, forever. No breakups. No drama for Finn. Or for any of us. It could be amazing."

I took a sip of my wine, letting the chilled liquid swirl on my tongue. "Yes. That's true. But after what happened before, I don't think it's fair to Finn for me to take that gamble. And honestly, I don't think I could handle losing Finn the way I lost Bella."

"Mrs. Peters," Finn said, running up to me after class.

I rolled my eyes good-naturedly. "Finn, for real. It's Ms. Peters."

"Oh, yeah. Sorry."

The kid was exceptionally bright. I'd known that from the start. Why he couldn't get that little bit of my name right was beyond me. "What's up? Did you have fun today?"

He raised a brow. "I know you want me to say yes, but no. Field hockey is *not* my thing. Sorry, not sorry."

I laughed. "That's fine, you're allowed to have preferences, as long as you give it a shot."

"So, uh, I wanted to tell you ..."

He looked up and closed one eye while he thought about what he wanted to say, and I fought back a giggle as I realized I'd seen his dad do the same thing. "Yes?"

"There's a big sale on groceries at the commissary today."

"Groceries? Like, all of them?"

He nodded, his eyes bright. "Yep. *Huge* sale. Great prices. You should definitely go there today after school so you can get some."

I narrowed my eyes at him and put my hands on my hips. "I don't have the right kind of ID to shop at the commissary. Sorry, Finn."

His big brown eyes widened. "What do you mean? You can get on base to teach here, why can't you shop here?"

"The commissary is only for people with a military ID, either active duty or dependent or former military. I have a Department of Defense ID that lets me teach here. See?" I held my ID badge between us from where it hung around my neck.

He looked closely at the ID and frowned deeply. "That doesn't seem very fair."

Ah, yes, Finn was a sucker for fairness. "I don't mind. I get lots of cool benefits being a Department of Defense teacher, and you get lots of cool benefits being a military dependent."

"Well," he said, then paused, thinking. "Um ..."

I tilted my head at him. "Is there a specific reason why you want me to go to the commissary today, Finn?"

"What? No? Why?"

"Just wondering."

The bell rang. "Oh, uh, time to go. See ya!"

I laughed as he ran away, looking back as he reached the door and giving me one last wave. I returned it, shaking my head at him.

After school, I couldn't help my curiosity. Even though I felt like a creepy stalker, I poked my head around the side of the building and checked to see who was waiting to pick up Finn that day. Sure enough, the tall, handsome, half-Irish dreamboat named Owen O'Malley stood there in his cammies looking like a snack.

I sighed. Why did he have to be so ... *everything*?

Finn ran into his waiting arms and hugged him tight. I watched as they headed for their car, then I hustled to mine in the teacher's lot nearby. I made the thirty second drive to the commissary. And just as I suspected, I saw them head into the store, hand in hand. Looked like there was a reason Finn wanted me to shop there today, after all. Just like there'd been a reason he'd wanted me to check out the new Starbucks that opened on base the day before. He was doing everything in his power to get us to run into each other. And it probably didn't help that I'd suggested we go to the beach for ice cream after the time with the paintings. That did nothing but confuse him. And me. And probably Owen, too.

I pulled out of the parking lot, a sinking feeling settling in my gut. This kid was worming his way into my heart. Little by little, day by day. And every time he did something like this to get me and his dad in the same place, I fell for both of them a little bit more.

OWEN

I put the weights on the ground next to my feet and stood, stretching my arms over my head. Spencer had spent his tax return creating a fancy home gym in his garage, and he'd invited me over to work out. It was a pretty sweet setup with a rack of dumbbells in varying weights from the lightest to accommodate Ellie's sets with more reps to the heavier weights that he wanted for his sets. There was a cage in the corner for pull-ups, squats, and a whole host of other full-body workouts. I was definitely impressed. Spencer didn't need to go to the gym at all with this situation in the garage. And now neither did I—perks of being his newfound brother.

Finn was inside watching TV with Ellie while we worked out, and I loved how attentive she was with him.

There was something about seeing his new family members take to him right away, and him to them, that made me even more grateful we'd decided to find them.

I took my role in Finn's life very seriously. I was his dad, yeah, but I was also his only living parent. Which made me try even harder to be everything to him. I wanted to be his friend, his confidant, the place he went for refuge when he was scared, and the first person he wanted to tell when something exciting happened. My mom picked up a lot of the slack with that because work prevented me from being there all the time, but now he also had an aunt, uncle, and grandpa, too.

"Oh, hey," I said, pulling out one of my earbuds and waving a hand for Spencer to do the same, "how's your plan going to get our parents together?"

Spencer snorted. "Like a charm. You don't know about their dates?"

My eyes widened. "Dates? As in, *plural*? They've gone out on more than one date? I knew they were talking but I didn't know they were actually *dating*."

"Yep."

I frowned. Why wouldn't she tell me? My mom had dated a few guys throughout my life and she'd never hidden them from me. Sure, she didn't introduce me to them until it got serious, but it wasn't necessarily a secret up until that point.

"Where? When?" I asked.

"I don't know specifics, but I know a couple times they went out for lunch."

While Finn was at school and I was at work. "Interesting."

"And did you guys have chili for dinner the other night?"

I narrowed my eyes at him. "Yes ..."

"How was it?"

"Good ..."

He snorted. "That's an award-winning Hawkins family recipe. He made her a pot of it."

My eyes bulged and shook it off. I should be happy for her, I knew. But still. I'd been so wrapped up in my own dating drama that I hadn't even noticed my mom was dating my ... dad.

"He said they're really hitting it off," Spencer continued, doing bicep curls with the thirty-five-pound weights in each hand.

I scratched my head. "Hey, can I ask you something?"

"Sure, what's up?"

"Does it bug you?"

"What?"

"You know, that your dad is seeing someone again ... after your mom ..."

Spencer nodded once in understanding. "Ah. Gotcha."

"I know it was a long time ago ..."

"Definitely a lot longer than three years."

My eyes flashed to his. "Do you think it's too soon for me to be thinking about that?"

Spencer held out his hands. "No, no. I didn't mean it like that. I figured that's why you were asking. Is this about Rachel?"

I shrugged. "I mean, she put the brakes on us, anyway, so I don't really know why I care. But yeah, I guess I'm kind of wondering about the perspective on the dad dating again after the mom passes away, from the kid's point of view. Even though I know you're not a kid anymore—you know what I mean."

"Yeah, I do," he replied. "If you want, I can talk to him about it. I don't have to say anything specific, but just kind of feel him out?"

I thought about his offer. Did I want that? I knew Finn wanted me to start dating Rachel, but she wasn't into the idea. Did that mean he wanted me to start dating other people, too? And if so, would that cause me to actively start doing it? I was always trying to make him happy, and if I found out that's what he wanted, I'd do my best to give it to him. On the other hand, was that a good reason to date? Shouldn't it be because I was ready to find someone and not because my eight-year-old wanted me to?

"Dude, I can see the steam coming out of your head while your wheels turn."

I chuckled. "It's a lot to think about."

"Yeah, I can imagine." Finished with his set, he put the weights back and toweled off his forehead. "For what it's worth, I think you should give it a shot with Rachel."

"What do you know about it?" I asked, raising a brow.

Spencer waved a hand. "Oh man, welcome to the group. We're all way too wrapped up in each other's business. I know you two went out a couple times. And I know you guys have kissed."

"*Eesh.*"

"I also know she broke it off with you when she found out you were Finn's dad. And I even know *why.*"

"Apart from the obvious awkwardness of dating your student's dad?"

"Yep."

I held out my arms. "Are you gonna tell me?"

Spencer laughed. "Word is she dated a student's dad a few years ago, and it didn't go well. I don't know details, so you should probably ask her, but maybe it would help if you had a conversation with her where you set yourself apart from the dude who did her dirty."

I considered this. "Yeah, maybe."

"That is, if you like her enough to try."

Thoughts of Rachel's pretty blue eyes, tan skin, and perfectly toned body filled my mind. She was obviously gorgeous, but that wasn't the only thing that drew me to her. She was also kind, funny, smart, *and* she played fantasy football. For our first date, she'd suggested a run, which was right up my alley. And then there was the easy way she seemed to make Finn laugh. Or the fact that her presence in our life could make us all healthier and more active, since she cared about that kind of stuff, too. Basically, she was amazing. I *definitely* liked her enough to try.

"I do."

The next day, I spent a little bit longer than necessary getting ready for the school's Breakfast with Dad event. I told myself I wanted to look presentable so Finn would be proud of his dad when he introduced me to his friends, but I knew he wouldn't care what I looked like. Nope, whether I wanted to admit it or not, it was because the event was being held in the gym, and the gym was the most likely place I'd find a certain PE teacher with a killer smile.

When we got to the school, Finn stayed pretty close to my side. He pointed out some of his other teachers and a few casual friends here or there, but he didn't seem too eager to leave my company for theirs. Used to him being shy in big crowds, I poked him lightly in the belly, making him laugh.

"You doing okay, bud?"

He shrugged. "Yeah. Why?"

"Just making sure."

I scanned the crowded room, but there was no sign of her. I shouldn't have gotten my hopes up. Why would she be at a Breakfast with Dad event for the third grade? She was the PE teacher for the whole school. Surely, she had better things to do than show up early and crash this party.

"Earth to Planet Dad," Finn said, waving a hand in front of my face. "Come in, Planet Dad."

"Sorry, what?"

"I *said*, there's a waffle bar over there. We should go make some."

"You don't even like waffles." I turned in the direction he was pointing, and my heart skipped a beat even as I rolled my eyes at Finn.

"Sure I do," he replied, grabbing my hand. "Let's go."

We made our way through the crowd to the long white table. There were platters with waffles stacked five or six high, surrounded by bowls of fruit, whipped cream, chocolate sauce, and other toppings. And standing behind the delicious spread with tongs in hand was Rachel Peters, the PE teacher who'd run away with my heart.

"Good morning, Finn," she said, all smiles for my boy. "And good morning, Mr. O'Malley."

I put a hand on my chest. "Ah, the *formalities*, Ms. Peters."

She winked at me, turning my blood to fire in my veins before turning back to Finn and asking how many waffles he wanted. I watched as she served up the heaping plate. He'd requested one waffle—that he likely wouldn't even touch—with a mound of strawberries, blueberries, whipped cream, and chocolate sauce drizzled on top. I shook my head at him as he took the plate with a huge grin.

"Dad, I'm gonna go grab a seat next to Nico over there." He tilted his head at a nearby table where some kids sat with their dads. "Take your time. I know how much you like ... waffles. Bye, Ms. Peters!"

He took off as fast as his little legs could take him while carrying a full plate, and I turned back to Rachel with a barely concealed smile. "Sorry about him."

"Oh, you mean sorry about the little trickster who just pretended he liked waffles?"

My mouth popped open in surprise. "How do you know he doesn't like waffles?"

"We were talking about the event in class yesterday. He said he didn't want to come to a breakfast thing because his dad always buys the best cereal anyway. Plus, he figured they'd only serve the healthy stuff that tasted like cardboard at a *school* event."

I choked out a laugh. "That sounds like Finn."

"Yep. Then I told him I'd be working the waffle table and he should come by and see me. Let's just say there was something about his face that told me he didn't like waffles. And yet, here you are."

"Here we are."

"Pretty smart kid you've got there."

She turned to the woman manning the waffle table with her and whispered that she'd be a minute. We stepped to the side of the table and I tucked my hands into my pockets, then pulled them back out. I needed something to do with them, so I picked up a baseball flyer from the table.

"Man, I really wish Finn would do this."

She arched a brow. "I've been working on him."

Of course she had. Because she was my freaking dream woman who not only cared about her own health and fitness, but also wanted to bring some of that out in my kid, who only ran if someone was chasing him. Even as the nerves swarmed in my gut like a hive of bees, I knew I had to take my shot. Like Spencer said, a conversation that told her I wasn't like the last dad she dated could go a long way.

"Do you get to come and go as you please?" she asked before I could say anything.

"What do you mean?"

She wrinkled her nose. "This might sound like I'm paying way too much attention to you ... but I've noticed you've been picking Finn up from school at like three thirty, and now here you are in civilian clothes like you don't even go here. I just wondered if your schedule was super flexible so you can do all of that. There usually aren't a lot of dads at pick-up, here on base or back in Texas. I'm starting to think those cammies are just for my benefit."

I wasn't much of a blusher, but I felt the heat rise up my cheeks. "Ah, yeah, I have a weird schedule. I alternate between a week of night crew and a week of day crew. If you see me picking up Finn, I'm on day crew. We get out at around two thirty. This week, I'm night crew, that's why I'm able to be here this morning."

"So, you'll go in around two thirty this afternoon and then what time are you off tonight?"

"Usually around eleven." I fidgeted with the flyer in my hands. Finn went through an Origami phase last year and my fingers started making a crane before I even realized what I was doing. "That's why I'm so glad to have my mom around. She's able to pick Finn up from school and do the whole dinner and bedtime story thing. I don't see much of him during my night crew weeks."

"I'm sorry. That's a bummer."

I shrugged. "Military life. Speaking of, how do you like teaching at a school on base? Pretty different from back home?"

"Much."

"How so?"

She looked up and blew out a breath. "Well, there are more kids in each class than there were back in Texas. So that's been interesting to get used to. Also having kids transferring in or moving away is new for me. Everyone at my school in Fort Worth was in it for the long haul, for the most part. We're only a few weeks into the school year, and I've already gained a couple new students—Finn included—and lost a few."

"Yeah, we tried to get here before the school year started, but there were a few delays on my end. Usually PCS season is over the summer though, so kids don't have to deal with that."

"PCS ... what does it stand for again?"

"Permanent change of station."

She arched a brow. "Doesn't *seem* very permanent."

I chuckled. "Well, three years is a lot more permanent than temporary in this world. Temporary orders could be days, weeks, or months. Accompanied or unaccompanied. By the family, that is."

"Wow. Sometimes I wonder if I'll ever understand all of this stuff. Little stuff and big stuff. That's another difference between teaching here versus teaching at a civilian school. I don't have the same kind of experiences as these kids, so it's hard to relate sometimes. I've got kids with moms or dads deployed who freak out in my class—understandably—because they miss them. All of the running around just kind of gives them an emotional outlet, and then before I know it, they've got tears. I don't think I went a week without my parents when I was a kid. My mom didn't even let me go to sleep-away camp."

I smiled, seeing how it could all feel very intense from the outside. "Yeah ... These kids sacrifice a lot."

"You all do. I guess I didn't realize how different it would feel until I was smack dab in the middle of family life on base."

"Do you think you could live this life?" I asked, unable to help myself. "Just out of curiosity."

Her head tilted to one side and her mouth quirked slightly. "I think that for the right guy, I can understand the draw. But that's purely theoretical."

I wanted to roll my eyes at her and her boldness that tortured me. Why did she have to make me feel like I could be the right guy for her if she wasn't ready to let herself go there? My mom's words flashed in my mind at the same time as Spencer's. I wasn't the kind of guy who gave up easily, and I needed to set myself apart from the guy she'd had a bad experience with.

"My turn for full disclosure," I started, then let out a breath. "I know you once dated a student's dad and it didn't go well."

Her eyes bulged. "You do, huh?"

"Yep. My source said something along the lines of, 'Welcome to the group, everyone's in everyone else's business.'"

Rachel let out a laugh, her head tilting back and her eyes bright. "I've noticed."

"I don't know details, though. About your ex, I mean."

"Are you asking for details?"

"Not unless you want to share them with me. Everyone has their stuff."

She blew out a breath and we both laughed awkwardly.

I looked down at the crane in my hand, moving my fingers over the wings as I spoke. "Was there a lot of drama involved last time you dated a student's dad?"

"Yep."

"And maybe some heartache for the kid, too?"

"Right again."

I met her eyes and held them steadily. "I don't know what kind of guy he was, or what kind of drama he caused, but I'm not him and I don't like drama. And the *last* thing I want to do is hurt Finn."

She stood straighter and crossed her arms over her chest. "I see."

"He likes you. *I* like you. And I think ... I could be wrong ... but maybe you like us, too."

Even though she tried to bite it back, she smiled. "Maybe."

"Look. I promise I'll respect your decision if you're not into it. But take it from me, having bad stuff in your past doesn't mean you should avoid taking risks in the future."

Her arms fell to her sides and her whole body seemed to relax from its guarded stance. I held the crane between us and watched her face as she slowly reached out and took it from my hand. Her gaze met mine and her lips twitched into a small smile.

It took everything I had not to kiss her right then and there in front of the whole third grade class. And their dads. It had been so long since I'd felt like this. As much as I hoped my little nugget of wisdom about the past and future would sway her to give us a chance, I knew she still might not want to go there again.

Realizing that she may shut me down and wanting to delay it out of self-preservation, I winked. "You don't have to answer me now. Think about it and let me know."

And with that, I tapped the crane on the head as she held it suspended between us and walked away.

"Hey, how was breakfast with Finn?" My mom asked as I walked in the door.

"Good. Also saw Rachel."

She wagged her eyebrows from her seat at the table, closing the magazine she was reading. "Oh? How did that go?"

I held out my hands. "We'll see. Hopefully she lets go of whatever's holding her back and gives me a shot. Can't force her to try."

"Well, I'm just happy to see you're not giving up on love, sweetheart."

I glared at her, crossing my arms over my chest. "Same here, *Mom*."

"And what is *that* supposed to mean?"

"Oh, I don't know, maybe the fact that you fed me and my son an award-winning, secret Hawkins family chili that your boyfriend made for you?"

Mom let out a big, full laugh. "It was pretty good though, wasn't it?"

"That is definitely not the point."

"What is the point, Owen? Do you think I should have told you that I was dating your father?"

I may have already known that she and Mike had been talking, but the verbal confirmation from her was still jarring. "Yes. I think you should have told me."

"And why is that, dear?"

I had no idea. "Because ... well ... because I care about you."

"Finn cares about me, too. Do you think I should tell him about my love life?"

I scoffed, taking a seat at the counter. "Of course not. He's a child. Plus, if he got all excited that you and his *new grandpa* were together and then something went wrong and you broke up, he'd just be disappointed."

She blinked at me. "Exactly."

"What? You're saying you didn't tell me because you didn't want me to get my hopes up and then get disappointed?"

"Owen. How many times did you wish for that very thing to happen when you were growing up?"

I rolled my eyes. "Mom. Come on. I'm an adult now."

"You'll always be my baby, remember?"

I couldn't help the chuckle that escaped me. "Ugh."

"Seriously, though. I didn't know if anything was going to come of it, and I've never made a habit out of telling you about my love life until there was something to tell. It's just not what we do. This isn't any different."

"It's a little different." I fidgeted with a piece of junk

mail on the counter. "I guess I'm worried about all of us being affected if it doesn't work out."

She smiled warmly at me, then crossed from the kitchen table to a barstool by my side. "Sweetheart, I promise. Mike and I are mature adults. If it didn't go well between us, we wouldn't let that effect any of the other relationships going on here. You'd still be able to continue building a connection with him and Spencer. And they'd still want to be in Finn's life. Nothing would have to change with any of that. And if it does work out between us, well, that's even better, right?"

I looked at her out of the corner of my eye, but didn't reply.

"Do you think you might be projecting a bit of your own worries onto me right now?"

"What, are you a shrink now?"

She made a face at me. "Shush. I know you better than you know yourself. And I think all this talk about dating Finn's teacher and how that will effect Finn if it doesn't work out might have something to do with your feelings about me and Mike."

"Or," I said, holding up a finger, "maybe we should both chill out with dating people who are close to Finn just in case it blows up in our faces."

She wrapped her arms around my shoulders. "God puts people in our lives however He sees fit. We don't get to choose how they're introduced to us, or when, or how long they *stay*. I feel good about my situation because I've prayed about it. Maybe you should, too."

I sighed. "Maybe I should. Anyway, I have to go. I'm meeting my buddy Noah at the gym. He goes during his workday because it's not as busy as when the after-work crowd is there."

"Sounds good," she replied, giving me one last squeeze before letting go. "I'm glad you're making friends here. I have a good feeling about San Diego for this little family of ours."

"Me too."

12

RACHEL

"**A**re you excited for the first day of practice today?" I asked after gym class, holding my breath while I waited for Finn's answer.

He rewarded me with a huge smile. "Yep. Are you ready for my dad to be a coach with you?"

"*What?*"

My chest tightened. Owen O'Malley was going to be the death of me. First, he knocks me off my feet by showing up to our fantasy football draft. Then, he fully secures my swooning with some amazing kisses at the beach. Next, he makes me regret all of my life choices for looking great in cammies while I'm trying to tell him I can't date him. And then finally, he made my knees weak with his smoldering eyes and dumb paper crane while asking if I'll give it a shot with him.

And I still hadn't given him an answer. There was no way I'd be able to coach baseball with him without making up my mind, and I bet he knew it, too.

"Yep. He signed up to coach," Finn explained. "He can only do it on the weeks he works day crew, though. He'll be at work during practice if he's on night crew."

I swallowed. "I'm sure that'll be fine. Will he be there today?"

"Yep. He's on days this week."

"Cool. And do you have everything you need for practice?"

"My dad took me shopping yesterday after school." He lowered his voice and looked around, almost as if he was sharing a secret with me that he didn't want anyone to know. "Getting all that cool new gear kind of made me excited about it."

I stifled a laugh. "Good, I'm glad. What did you get?"

"Well, he got me a glove, a ball, and a bat," he said, counting on his fingers as he listed each item. "The bat is *really* light. The first time I swung it, I *threw* it."

My eyes bulged in surprise to match his. "Uh-oh. Did you break anything?"

"Not yet. Dad says it's only a matter of time, though."

I chuckled. "What else did you get?"

"He got me some baseball pants and socks and

shoes. And he's making me wear a hat. But I'm really not a big fan of hats. They bother my head."

"You'll get used to it, O'Malley. It's a baseball thing."

He rolled his eyes but not without a classic Finn smile. "If you say so."

"Did you write your name on your ball, bat, and glove?"

"Nope, should I?"

I nodded. "Yes. It'll be easier to keep track of your stuff that way."

"Okay, thanks." The bell rang and Finn waved as he ran off. "See ya later."

I watched him go for a moment before turning to clean up the gym from the obstacle course I'd set up for his class. Finn had loved it, which was my prayer when I'd seen it coming up in my lesson plans earlier that week. I was starting to get to know which activities he'd like and which ones would make him nervous.

Independent activities like going through an obstacle course were always easier for him than a team sport. He didn't like the pressure of potentially causing his team to lose because of something he did wrong. Heaven forbid we did a relay race.

I knew baseball would be fine during practice and then get hairy during games, but I'd had weeks of being his PE teacher to help me figure out how to coach him. And Owen has had eight years of being his dad, so between the two of us, hopefully Finn would wind up loving it.

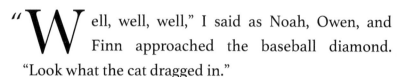

"Well, well, well," I said as Noah, Owen, and Finn approached the baseball diamond. "Look what the cat dragged in."

"Hey, Rach," Noah said, adjusting the bag on his shoulder and nodding to the coach's bench. "I'll go check in."

"Sounds good."

I'd found out at the fantasy draft that Noah was a high school baseball star who turned down a scholarship to join the military. I had no idea why. As much as I loved my country, I cringed at the idea of turning down a full ride to college where I'd get to play sports and get a degree for free. But it wasn't my business. Questionable decision making aside, once he'd told me how much he missed playing, I had to tell him about the opportunity to coach on base.

Owen had a wide smile for me as Noah left. "I've always wanted to coach baseball for my kid."

"But I've never done baseball," Finn said, angling his head extra far back to see his dad from under his ball cap.

"Exactly," Owen replied.

"Glad to have you both on board," I said. "Finn, why don't you go join the rest of the team over there."

He eyed the eleven other players as they sat in the grass, one leg bent and the other extended, reaching out to touch their toes. "What are they doing?"

"Stretching."

"Yes, but why?"

I bent my knee and held my foot against my backside. "Stretching allows the muscles to loosen up and get warm. That way when they face resistance while you're being active, they go with the flow and you have less of a chance of getting injured."

"They look pretty flexible. I don't think I'm that flexible." He squinted up at me, the bright sunlight pouring over him.

Unsurprised by his hesitancy to participate, I flashed him a smile. "Finn, blessed are the flexible, for they will never be bent out of shape."

Owen rewarded my corny joke with a chuckle, but Finn merely looked between us with a frown. "Bent out of shape, how? Is this going to be dangerous?"

"Oh, Finn. Just go do what the other kids are doing," Owen said, pointing to the team. We laughed as we watched him run over and sit down. "He's a trip."

"So are you." I playfully pushed his arm, not disliking the feel of his hard bicep under my hand.

"Do you have anything you want to tell me, *Ms.* Peters?"

I bit my lip, knowing it was time to lay my cards on the table. I had to give him my answer about whether or not I'd break my hard-and-fast rule about not dating a student's dad. I took a deep breath.

"Kids, Pete's going to keep doing your stretches. Coaches, let's circle up," Len, the team's head coach called to the group.

"Saved by the bell," I said to Owen before turning and jogging over to Len.

The smattering of full-time coaches and parent volunteers formed a loose circle around Len. He was employed by Little Trooper League and had two other guys with him as part of the staff. Then there was me as a part-time addition, Noah as a baseball-loving volunteer, and several hands-on parents like Owen. I felt heat radiating off of Owen as he stood next to me, his large arms crossed over his broad chest, his elbow grazing my upper arm.

"Thanks for coming," Len addressed us. "My hope is that this is a great year for these seven-, eight-, and nine-year-olds, with no injuries and plenty of fun."

My eyes darted to Finn and sure enough, he'd been half stretching, half listening to Len briefing us coaches. I winked at him to reassure him, and he gave me a look that was halfway in the smiling camp and halfway to a grimace.

"Today's plan is to start off with stretching, as the kids are already working on with my guy, Pete. They're going to work on stationary stretches and also some dynamic stretches to get their blood pumping."

The sun beat down on my shoulders, and I wondered idly if I'd remembered to put sunblock on when I'd gotten out of the shower that morning. My eyes wandered to Owen's arm, then quickly away. I'd caught sight of quite the farmer's tan under the hem of his short-sleeved shirt.

I laughed to myself as I remembered seeing all of the Marines with their shirts off when we'd gone to the beach as a big group. Most of them had the same stark contrast between the skin that hid under their uniforms and the skin on their arms that stuck out from the sleeves of their rolled cammies. Too bad Owen hadn't been in San Diego yet when we'd made that beach trip, I wouldn't have minded seeing him with his shirt off.

"Coach Peters, is it? Ground balls or fly balls?" Len asked.

I shook my head. "I'm so sorry, what?"

"I asked if you'd rather throw ground balls or fly balls to the players. We're going to break up into groups and have the outfielders practice catching fly balls, the infielders catch ground balls, and the batters will take turns hitting off the tees and live throws."

"Got it, sorry. I'll do the fly balls," I replied.

Owen grunted next to me, but I didn't get a chance to ask him what the noise was for because Len turned to him and told him to do ground balls. After all of the coaches and parents had their assignments, we split up and got started. I grabbed some kids and headed for the outfield, Owen grabbed a few for the infield, and the rest moved into position to alternate at bat with Noah. Finn made sure to join his dad's group, which I was grateful for. Ground balls would likely be the easiest thing for him to try first.

As I lobbed the balls in the air for my outfielders to practice catching, I gave them a few pointers. A couple of the kids struggled with keeping their gloves wide enough to catch the ball, so I instructed them to catch a few light ones without the glove so they could see how to keep their hands soft when catching.

After a moment of watching that pay off, Owen backed up to where I was standing near second base and nodded at me. "Hey, cool tip. Think it'll work for these ground balls?"

"It should. Give it a shot."

He instructed Finn and the other two boys to take off their gloves. I continued throwing fly balls for my group but kept an ear out for Owen's instruction since he was new to coaching. He did a good job explaining it to the kids, especially Finn, and I watched his face light up as the kids all caught on a lot better when they put their gloves back on.

"Nice, thank you," Owen said, getting closer to me again. "Did you coach back in Texas, too?"

"Yep," I replied, lobbing up another light one for one of my kids who wasn't as experienced as the others.

"Question. Why isn't Coach having us hit these grounders and fly balls to the kids instead of throwing them?"

I raised a brow at him. "What's up, Mickey, you think you can hit a consistent and intentional grounder every single time you get up to bat?"

"Mickey, as in, 'Oh Mickey, you're so fine'?"

"No, as in Mickey Mantle."

He sighed and launched another grounder. "Bummer. But I don't know, I've never tried."

"Well, we throw grounders and fly balls so they get practice catching as many of them as possible before Coach blows the whistle and they switch."

As if on cue, Coach blew the whistle and told everyone to rotate to the next station. This brought Finn to my station, and I high fived him as he jogged over. "How's it going?"

"Good," he panted. "I think I'm getting the hang of it."

I wagged my eyebrows at Owen over Finn's head, knowing he heard that. "Good, I'm glad. Now scoot out there, and I'll teach you how to catch a fly ball."

An hour later, Finn was completely wiped. Even though he seemed to be so tired he could barely move his feet, he wore a huge grin on his face.

"Thanks for today," Finn said, hugging me around the waist.

"You did really great. I'm proud of you." I returned his sweaty hug then waved as he ran off to go catch up to his dad and Noah, who were talking quietly and looking over here.

Owen bent down to say something to him, then Finn took off for the parking lot with Noah. Owen walked up to me, hands in the pockets of his athletic shorts. His smile was slow and easy, and my heart skipped a beat—or two, or seven—as he got closer.

"Where are they going?"

Owen looked over his shoulder and we watched as Noah walked Finn to the car his grandma had pulled up in right as they got to the parking lot. "My mom just got done at the commissary and she said she'd come grab him and get the nighttime routine started."

I frowned. "I wish I could shop at the commissary.

Finn tried to get me to go there once when you guys were going. He told me they were having a huge sale on *all* of the groceries. But I had to tell him civilians aren't allowed to shop there."

"Wow," Owen said, tossing his head back and laughing. "Uh, yeah, my mom has a dependent ID now. It was easier to make her a dependent after ... after Rebecca passed."

Desperate to find something to show him I could be mature talking about her, I smiled. "It's so great that your mom is such a big help with him. I'm sure he loves having her close."

"He definitely does. He seemed like he had fun out there today. I'd be lying if I said I wasn't nervous going into it."

"I was, too," I admitted. "But yes, he did great. There was one moment where he had a minor freak-out."

"Ah, yeah, I was going to ask you about that. What happened? I couldn't hear from where I was."

I dug my toe in the sand. "Oh you know, the usual for Finn. He was nervous about what would happen in a high stakes championship game if the bases were loaded and there were two outs and he was the one up to bat."

Owen laughed, a hand on his broad chest. "Of course."

"I told him they'd have to practice really hard as a

team to ever get to a high stakes championship game, so
he shouldn't worry about it. If they made it that far,
chances are he was probably able to hit that game-
winning run."

"You know exactly how to handle him," he
observed.

"Finn isn't a hard kid to understand. I mean, he's
complex and smart, don't get me wrong, I'm just saying ...
his needs are easy to understand. He wants to know the
rules of the game so he knows what's expected of him.
And that means he wants everyone else to play by those
same rules, so he knows what to expect from them."

"And fairness, above all, is key," Owen added.

"Exactly," I replied, staring up into his blue eyes and
losing myself in the way he seemed to hang on my every
word about Finn. "So, uh, now that Grandma took him
home to start the bedtime routine, does that mean you
might be free for dinner?"

His eyebrows shot up to his hairline. "Dinner? As in,
two friendly coaches grabbing a bite after practice?"

I shook my head. "Nope."

Owen looked around, so I did, too. The other kids
and parents and coaches had pretty much cleared out,
so we were nearly alone at the baseball diamond. I
couldn't help but let my eyes wander back to him, to his
lips, then to his eyes—which were staring back at me.

Without giving me enough time to take in a breath, he pulled me into his arms, crushing me against his chest. His lips glided over mine with more tenderness than expected given how eagerly his hands slid over my arms and upper back.

I lifted up on my toes, needing to be even closer to him. He grabbed me around the waist, his fingers pressing into me as he lifted me easily. I wrapped my legs around his waist and locked my ankles, pulling back from the kiss and breathing heavily.

"Hi," I said, laughing, eye level with him as he held me.

"Hi."

"So, we're going to do this?"

He shrugged, still not putting me back on the ground. "I think it would be fun."

"And you're sure Finn will be okay?"

The heat I'd seen in his gaze gave way to something more resembling affection. Confidence. Resolve. "Yes. I am. And the fact that you care means more to me than you'll ever know."

I couldn't help the wide grin that spread over my face. "Okay. I'm in."

"Yeah?"

"Yeah. Moving to San Diego was a big risk for me. And what you said last week about not letting bad stuff prevent me from taking risks reminded me that I wasn't that kind of person, anyway. Why start now?"

Owen grinned, and rather than speaking, he chose to close the conversation with another one of his fantastic kisses.

13

OWEN

"I'm glad I'm able to eat at the food court even though I can't shop at the commissary. I try to pack healthy lunches, but sometimes I'm in the mood for something fried." Rachel shoved a fry in her mouth and moaned, making me laugh.

"These are the best fries, for sure."

"Agreed." She took a sip of her Coke. "Thanks for meeting me for lunch. How's your morning been?"

"Good, so far. Nothing exciting. Yours?"

She rolled her eyes. "Actually, I had a kid fall off the bleachers in first period. Ambulance came and everything. Poor thing broke his arm."

I'd just taken a bite of my burger, so I replied with a mumbled tone that sounded like, "*Seriously?*"

"Yep. I felt so bad. Plus, you know, a compound fracture is never pretty."

"Ugh."

"Not the best lunchtime conversation, though," she said with a laugh. "My bad."

"That's okay, I have a pretty strong stomach. I must get it from my mom. She's a nurse."

"Ah, I can only imagine," she said, wrinkling her nose in a way that made me want to reach out and tap on it with my finger. She had such a sweet face, always perfectly on display since her hair was always pulled back in a high ponytail. "Speaking of your mom and dad, how's all of that going?"

I shrugged a shoulder. "They're officially dating, in the open. Finn is aware of it and excited about it. I hope it goes well."

"Me too." She eyed me carefully. "And how is it with getting to know him and Spencer as your dad and brother?"

"It's a lot easier than I expected it to be. I love having a brother. I've had friends that have felt like brothers, which is probably normal being a Marine. But it's cool actually having a brother."

"What do you mean about it being easier than you expected? Did you think it would be hard?"

"Well, don't get me wrong, when I was a kid, I dreamed of finding a ready-made family to slip right into. Finally find where I belonged, you know? But the older I got, the less I thought about it like that. It was more like, someday maybe I'll show up on this guy's doorstep and be like *ta-da.*"

Rachel laughed as I held my arms out and wiggled my fingers to punctuate my last remark.

"Anyway," I went on, "it's so wild to think that I showed up, said ta-da, and now we're like a big happy family who gets together every weekend—or more. It feels ... never mind."

"What?" she prompted, taking a big bite of her burger.

"It's cheesy."

She narrowed her eyes at me. "Tell me."

"It feels like an old dream ..."

"Coming true?" she finished for me, a wry smile on her lips.

"Yeah, I guess."

"You're right," she said, frowning playfully. "That's way too cheesy. I can't even."

I threw a fry at her. "You made me tell you."

"Yeah, yeah. For real, though, I'm really happy for you. And for Finn. It was just you, Finn, and your mom before?"

A familiar darkness settled over me and I swallowed it back. "Yeah, after Rebecca passed. Her family wasn't very involved when she was alive, and they really distanced themselves from us after she died. It was weird. And my mom doesn't really have any family."

"Owen, I'm sorry. I know we've talked about her here and there, but I've never asked ... how did Rebecca die?"

"Hodgkin's lymphoma," I replied, feeling the story making its way from where it was buried deep within me so I could lay it out for her. "At first, she started losing a lot of weight. She joked that it was her baby weight coming off years later, but it was pretty drastic. Then, she started getting sick all the time. Her lymph nodes got really big, but we didn't know anything about it and thought it was because she was sick a lot. She always said she was fine, that it was just a cold. Long story short, eventually we found out it was the cancer preventing her body from fighting off infections. She was always so tired. Anyway, she tried chemo, made a great effort. But like I mentioned that day at the beach, she passed away about two years after we got the diagnosis."

Rachel reached across the picnic table and took my hand. "I'm so sorry, Owen."

"Thank you." I was grateful that she didn't feel the need to say more. That was enough.

～

"Welcome, welcome, come on in."

I heard my mom greeting someone at the door, and I couldn't help the way my heart picked up speed at the thought of it being Rachel. I craned my neck around the corner, then my shoulders sagged when it was only Spencer and Ellie entering my house.

"Oh, hey," I deadpanned.

Spencer scoffed. "Well, hello to you, too, *brother*."

Ellie swatted him on the arm. "He's excited to see Rachel. Leave him be."

"*Shh*. Finn doesn't know we're a thing." My eyes darted around for my son, finding him out back with Mike, tossing a baseball.

Spencer followed my gaze and grinned. "Is that Finn or one of those changeling things? When I met that kid, he had the hand-eye coordination of a bat. The blind, flying-mammal kind, that is, not the sports kind."

"You're so funny." Ellie rolled her eyes at her husband as he made a swinging motion with his arms and chuckled at me. "Looks like baseball is going well. How long has he been doing it?"

"Two weeks now." Rachel joined us in the kitchen with my mom in tow, nodding at Spencer and Ellie. "Hey, guys."

Everyone greeted Rachel, and my chest warmed when her eyes lit up with a special smile for me. Finn apparently saw her through the window since he ran into the house, leaving Mike standing in the small yard, glove in hand, scratching his head. Finn launched himself into Rachel's waiting arms.

"Hi, Ms. Peters," he said.

"Hi, Finn." She smiled at me over his head. "Having a good weekend so far?"

"Yeah. Grandpa Mike took me fishing at Lake Cuyamaca."

"Ooh, where's that?" Rachel asked.

"It's up in the mountains over by Julian," Mike replied, coming in through the back door. "And if you don't know where that is, let's just say it's about an hour from here."

Rachel pointed. "Got it. I can't wait to do some more exploring. I've been here a few months, but I feel like I've barely scratched the surface. I didn't realize there were mountains and lakes for fishing around here. I pretty much only thought about deep-sea fishing or something else ocean related."

"San Diego has a lot to offer besides the beach," Mike said. "When Spencer was Finn's age, we used to go camping, horseback riding, hiking, fishing ... you name it, we did it. Right, Spence?"

"Yeah," he replied. "It was great."

Even though Mike had already turned away and continued talking to Rachel, I noticed Spencer smile sadly and look down. Ellie patted his hand where it rested on the counter. When Spencer had been Finn's age, his mom was still healthy and happy. They probably had such a good life at that time, exactly like I'd had with my wife and son before Rebecca got sick. And then, out of nowhere, it had all changed. Those trips probably became few and far between for Spencer, if ever again.

I knew that Mike had really checked out after his wife died. He'd been gone a lot before, and then continued to be gone a lot after. Being that I'd lived through a similar thing as a husband and father, I couldn't imagine doing that to Finn. Finn was all I had left of Rebecca after she passed, so if anything, there were times I worried I was smothering the poor kid. But I hadn't grown up with a dad, so that might explain why I'd go a little overboard.

I was pretty conflicted about how I felt about Mike because of this, but I tried not to let it ruin my own relationship with him or get in the way of the one he was building with Finn.

My mom helped a lot to remind me that people make mistakes and it's not our job to judge them or stop them from making amends, if that's what they felt called to do. And considering the attentiveness Mike has showed all of us since we'd met, he seemed to be on a mission to do just that.

"I caught a surgeon today," Finn said, vying for Rachel's attention.

"Sturgeon, buddy," Mike gently corrected him. "You caught a *sturgeon*."

"Oh, right. I thought surgeon was a weird name for a fish." He frowned. "Actually, *sturgeon* is a weird name for a fish, too."

We all laughed and small conversations broke out as everyone dished up their plates of food and settled in to eat. It was a buffet-style meal that my mom had prepared with Mike's help. It was weird watching them pass dishes to everyone and be perfect hosts together, in my house, with my kid. Not to mention my new brother and sister-in-law. Incorporating Rachel into the mix added a whole other level to the Norman Rockwell moment. She seemed to fit here with us, and we all seemed to fit together. Looking at it all from the outside in, you'd never know most of us met such a short time ago.

After dinner, I took advantage of the distraction Finn caused with wanting to help do the dishes and pulled Rachel into the hallway.

"Hey," I said, kissing her lightly on the forehead. "I missed you."

"I literally just saw you at breakfast this morning."

I shrugged. "Yeah, true. Thank goodness for that fishing trip so we could sneak away."

"About that," Rachel said, taking my hand in hers and holding it between us, "when do you think we should tell him we're dating? It's been two weeks of texting, talking on the phone, going on runs, meeting up for lunch during the week ..."

"And it's been great," I said. "I've really liked getting to know you."

"Me too. But now I'm at your *house*, Owen. We had dinner—all together. We should probably tell him about us and then have a talk with him about keeping it hush-hush at school."

"Do we need to keep it hush-hush at school? Didn't you say it wasn't a policy with the school, just something you didn't want to do?" I asked. She looked at our joined hands and wouldn't meet my eyes, so I put my finger under her chin and brought her face up to look at me. "Rach, talk to me."

"I've been trying not to dwell on the past because I know you're not *him* and it's not the same situation, but the administration gave me a hard time even though it wasn't an actual policy. And so did the other parents. It was such a mess."

I sighed. "So, what's your plan? Tell Finn about us, and then tell him to keep it a secret? Because I'm not sure how he'll do with that."

"Maybe we should have thought about that sooner."

"I'm great at secrets," a small voice whispered from behind me, making me jump.

I closed my eyes and let my shoulders fall, but didn't turn. "*Finn.*"

Rachel covered her mouth with her hand to stifle her laugh and tried to put on a serious face to match my own. It wasn't working.

Finn weaseled his way between us and his small face appeared, doing his best to look angelic and innocent. I glanced between him and Rachel, who was failing hard at containing her giggles. This made Finn beam up at me.

"Finn," I started again, "how many times do I have to tell you not to eavesdrop?"

He tapped his finger on his chin. "Maybe one more time?"

This made Rachel bend over in a fit of laughter, her long ponytail falling over her shoulder as she tickled Finn. They squealed and ran around, laughing, and as I watched him try to escape her using every evasive tactic in his book, I couldn't help the wide smile plastered on my face. This thing with Rachel was new, sure, but it had been at least five years since Rebecca was able to run around and play with Finn like this. He likely didn't even remember it. If Rachel and I worked out, he'd get to have this again. He'd get to have a mother figure who also loved to have fun and run around with him. And I'd have someone to share my life with.

I looked up at my mom. She stood in the kitchen watching Rachel and Finn play with tears in her eyes. She was probably having similar thoughts. I thought I might catch her eye to let her know we were on the same page, but then I saw Mike head over to where she stood and casually slip an arm around her waist. He gave her a companionable squeeze. Could it really be true that moving to San Diego had brought love for me and Finn, as well as my mom?

14

RACHEL

"This is nice." I squeezed his strong hand in mine as we walked down the beach, the early-morning sun casting a golden glow over the sand under our feet.

Owen took a sip of his coffee and then smiled down at me. "It is."

We'd planned to come to the beach for a run as usual, but somehow, it turned into strolling along the shore with coffee in hand. I didn't mind, it was the perfect pace for a Sunday morning. And after staying at his house watching movies with Finn and the rest of the family until midnight the night before, I was grateful for the coffee.

"What's your plan for today?" he asked.

"I figured I'd do some laundry, watch church online,

maybe go to the gym. Especially since we picked coffee over running this morning."

He chuckled. "We go to the church in Tierrasanta. Finn loves the children's ministry. Mom invited Mike."

"Oh, wow. He doesn't normally go to church, right?"

"Not from what Spencer's said. He seemed pretty surprised when he found out Mike was going, actually."

Diane and Mike had seemed pretty cozy the night before at dinner. Owen had told me about Spencer's plan to get them together, and it looked like it was working. Though, if I were being honest, I had a feeling he hadn't needed to work that hard to make it happen. They seemed like they were made for each other.

"Well, that's great. I hope he has one of those moments you know? Like the *ah-ha, I'm meant to be here* moments."

Owen squeezed my hand. "Me too. Hey, uh, would you want to come with us, too? Now that the cat's out of the bag."

I grinned, remembering Finn eavesdropping on our conversation about whether or not we should tell him about us. Then the way his smug little smile appeared later in the evening when we'd sat him down on the patio and told him we were a thing. The little stinker detailed several examples that we hadn't even been aware of in the little matchmaking scheme he'd orches-trated. And we'd told him about the stuff like the time he tried to get me to shop at the commissary when we'd seen right through him. It had been a really sweet conversation that I knew we'd treasure forever. You know, if we lasted forever, of course.

Nerves swam in my belly. I'd loved getting closer to Owen over the last two weeks. There was something so exciting about our lunch dates during the week or early-morning runs before school and work. Whenever we could fit time in, that wouldn't arouse suspicion in Finn, we did. And it was great. But now that—as he said —the cat was out of the bag ... how would dating feel? With Finn knowledgeable of our relationship, it stood to feel a lot less like two people at the beginning of their courtship and a lot more like a family unit on family outings. Less time for just us two, more time with all three of us.

"You look a little conflicted. What's up?" he asked.

I sighed. "I'd love to go to church with you guys."

"But?"

"I think we should talk about some ground rules if we're going to go public with our relationship."

He scratched his head. "Ground rules?"

"Yes. We didn't tell Finn to keep us a secret at school. I understand why you don't think that would be good for him, so fine. We won't. But we can't be super obvious at school, either."

"And what does super obvious look like?"

I rolled my eyes. "Oh you know, kissing, holding hands, being all lovey-dovey."

He tugged on my hand to bring me to a stop, pulling me close against him. The ocean breeze blew my hair around my face, so he reached up and tucked a few loose strands back behind my ear as he looked down at my face. Slowly, he brought his face down to mine, his lips lightly dusting a trail from my forehead, to my temple, to my cheek.

I closed my eyes, fully immersing myself in the clean scent of him mixed with the salty air surrounding us. Finally, his lips landed on mine, and the soft kiss was enough to make my knees weak and my mind muddy. After a moment, he pulled back, resting his forehead on mine.

"Is that the kind of lovey-dovey thing we should avoid at school?" he asked, a playful smile on his full lips.

"Yes," I replied. "You can't make me feel like that while I'm supposed to be an authority figure to hundreds of kids."

"Well, I have good news. Public displays of affection are not allowed on base." He took my hand again, and we continued walking down the beach. We passed a trash can and threw away our empty paper cups.

"Really?"

"Yep. One of the many things I'm not going to love about living on base, now that I have you."

I laughed. "What is there not to love? It's like a cute little town, protected from the craziness of the world. You have everything you need without ever leaving the base. Shopping, food, gas, parks, a pool, even a movie theater. I'm jealous."

Owen sighed dramatically. "Yes, yes, all of that is great. But you can never escape the Marine Corps. If you want to leave the house *for any reason*, you need to have a shave and make sure you're wearing proper civilian attire. Even to check the mail, since I need to go down the street to do it."

"Even to check the mail?"

"Yep. Technically, if you leave your house at all you're supposed to have a fresh shave."

I wrinkled my nose. "So restrictive."

"It's the military."

We laughed, and I bumped him with my shoulder. "What's proper civilian attire?"

"Always having a belt on, no basketball shorts unless you're actively working out, no tank tops—"

I snorted, then waved a hand in front of my face. "Sorry."

"What?" He eyed me. "What's so funny?"

I let go of his hand and turned around, walking backwards in front of him. "I was gonna say I could tell by your farmer's tan that you're not allowed to wear tank tops."

He scowled playfully. "Oh, you take that back."

"I will not," I said, laughing and picking up speed.

He charged after me so I turned around and ran, smiling wide and dodging him as he grabbed for me. Finally, he caught me around the waist, and planted a loud kiss on my mouth. "What are your other ground rules?"

"We need to make sure Finn knows he still has to call me Ms. Peters at school even if he can call me Rachel when we're all together."

"Makes sense."

"And I'm sorry if this sounds weird, but dating a single dad is a lot different than dating any other guy."

He glanced down at me as we walked along in the sand. "How so?"

"Have you, um, dated anyone since your wife passed?"

"No, I haven't."

I swallowed. I'd struck out on love so many times in the last three years alone, and in all of that time he'd been grieving his wife and trying to get to a point where he could finally date again. And now he was, *with me*. I hated the idea of us not working out, not only because of how I'd feel about it, but also because of how crushed he and Finn might be since this was the first time they'd opened their hearts up to another woman. But I was getting ahead of myself.

"I'm ready, though," he said, squeezing my hand.

"I'm glad," I replied. "But um, there's a level of seriousness that happens right at the beginning when there's a kid involved. Because I'm not just dating you with the end goal of finding love and starting a family. You already have a family that I'm stepping into."

He stopped walking and stuffed his hands in his pockets. "Does that make you uncomfortable?"

"Honestly? It does." His eyes flew to mine, and I held up my hands. "I don't want to step into your family and then if something happens, it hurts more than just us. It hurts Finn, too."

He relaxed a little, but his eyes were still wary.

"Also," I went on before he could say anything, "that was a big part of my issue last time. I felt like I'd stepped into kind of a second mom role with my ex's little girl. And then when we broke up, it felt like I was losing someone who meant more to me than I even knew how to explain at that time. I really, really care about Finn. Part of why I'm so scared to be with you is because I'm scared to lose him."

There was a long pause while he looked at me, his gaze full of emotion. "I'm glad you care about him. I know Finn wasn't even in the picture at first ... but once he was, part of why I'm falling for you is how you are with him."

"You're falling for me?" I asked, my voice barely audible over the sound of the waves behind me.

"Of course, I am. And if you can't tell that, then I'm going to need to step my game up a bit."

"I'm falling for you, too." I admitted, loving the way his eyes changed in that moment, like hope and excitement and even desire all swirled into one.

He cleared his throat and looked around, nodding and waving at a random couple who jogged by us. "Also, Spencer had a little heart-to-heart with Finn about me dating again."

"He did?"

"Yep. We pretty much knew he wanted it to happen with all of his little tricks to get us to hang out. But I guess he went on and on to Spencer about how perfect we are for each other. He's falling for you, too, Rach. This is a good thing we have going on here."

"So, I should get out of my head about the ground rules and the nerves about it ending badly and just go with it?" I asked, not without humor.

He reached out, placing a tender hand on my waist, pulling me closer. "It's taken me a long time to get to a place where I was willing to let another woman into my life. And Finn's. I'm not doing it lightly."

I stood on my tiptoes and gave him a quick kiss on the cheek. "Okay."

"Okay. So, no more ground rules? And you'll come with us to church later?"

"Well, since the PDA rule is a Marine Corps thing anyway, I guess just the one about him not calling me Rachel at school. Or baseball practice."

"Deal."

And because it seemed necessary, we sealed it with yet another perfect kiss.

15

OWEN

I crossed my arms over my chest and smiled as I watched Mike trying to teach Finn how to play golf. MCAS Miramar Memorial Golf Course was right on base, offering free rounds of golf to active duty members on Tuesday evenings as part of their quality of life improvement plan for Marines. Free or not, old vets would come from all over to play there and talk about the good ole days in the San Diego sun. I liked a lot of sports, but golf wasn't one of them. That being said, Spencer and Mike invited us, so here we were. Bonding with the guys.

"He's doing great," Spencer observed. "Maybe golf will be his thing."

I raised a brow. "Maybe."

"You definitely made him seem a lot less athletic than he actually is."

I thought about that for a minute before responding. Surely, it couldn't be because I didn't know my son as well as I thought I did. When Finn was a toddler, he loved to play with cars. But he didn't drive them around or have races with them, like I had when I was little. Instead, he'd lined them up in rows by color and type of vehicle. He was obsessed with categorizing them as a collection, not using them as a vehicle.

Even before he could read, he would pore over books for hours, just looking at the pictures. Mostly nonfiction, too. He liked books about animals or weather systems. My mom would take him to the library and he'd bring home armfuls of books to read on the couch with Rebecca, since that's pretty much all she could do at that time. If she was too tired to read to him, he'd look at the pictures and ask her endless questions until someone told him to let her rest. Then he'd look at the pictures in silence, trying to read, and eventually wound up teaching himself how.

I'd always encouraged him to go outside and play, but he never wanted to. He just wanted to stay inside and be near her. Then after she passed, at some point, he'd started escaping into video games. My mom said he still loved to read, and she encouraged me to monitor his screen time, but playing his game console and strategizing to win role-playing games became his number one hobby.

Had I made a mistake somewhere along the line? Should I have put my foot down and insisted he sign up for a sport? Should I have not given him the option to read a book or play a video game instead? I'd always figured I needed to let him be happy, considering what he was going through. But should I have stepped in and forced him to go outside and get some fresh air? Ever since we'd arrived in San Diego and physical activity had become more of a priority—largely thanks to Rachel—he'd been thriving. Guilt settled deep within me. What had I done to him while I was so busy grieving?

"Hello?" Spencer said, waving a hand in front of my face. "Where did you go?"

"Sorry."

He patted me on the shoulder. "You've got that look."

"What look?"

"It's something my dad does. Who knows, maybe I do it, too. It's like a faraway look. I always figure he's back in the past somewhere when he gets like that. Thinking about my mom. Thinking about me. The mistakes he's made."

I shuddered. Sometimes talking to Spencer was jarring. Knowing my kid—a kid who also lost his mom at a young age—was going to grow up and be able to notice stuff like that about me was a hard pill to swallow.

"It's okay," Spencer said. "It's probably normal."

Something he'd said hit home for me, though, so I risked a glance at his face. "What did you mean by thinking about the mistakes he made?"

"Well, we've already talked a lot about how checked out he was as a dad after she died. I think sometimes it eats away at him. But look at him now. He's great with your kid. And we've literally never had a better relationship than we do now that I'm a Marine. It is what it is. And you're clearly miles ahead of him. With Finn, that is. I don't know if you need to hear it or what, but you're doing a great job with him. Take it from someone who knows."

My throat tightened with emotion, so I gave him a small smile and nodded. "Thanks."

"It's been cool hanging out like this."

"Yeah, it has." I was telling the truth. Just as I'd told Rachel when she asked once, I really liked having a brother. And a dad. I'd been hanging out with both of them enough to realize how much I'd been missing. I knew in theory before this, of course, but now I really knew.

"And um, how's it all going with Rachel?"

I chuckled, glad for the subject change. "Great. We're coming up on a month of dating now."

"Wow. Time flies."

"It does." I scratched my head. "She's great. Finn loves her, so that's huge. We're apparently going to do family costumes for Halloween, so we're going to go pick them out this weekend."

"So you're saying it's getting serious."

"Clearly."

He laughed. "That's good, man. I'm happy for you."

"Thanks."

"Do you think you're gonna ... you know ...marry her? I mean, you probably jump from A to Z when there's a kid involved, right?"

I chuckled. "You gonna give me some advice there, little brother?"

Spencer brushed off his shoulder. "Yeah, well, I've got a pretty good thing going."

"It seems like you do."

He dug his toe in the dirt near the tree we stood under. "Ellie's pregnant, actually."

My head whipped in his direction, my mouth wide. "Ellie's pregnant?"

"Yep." He looked up at me, and my confident, goofball of a half-brother was white as a ghost.

"Are you scared?"

He blew out a breath. "Heck yeah, I'm scared. I'm terrified."

"Aw, man. It's okay. It's more than okay." My heart squeezed for him, almost like I was talking to a childlike version of him and not the adult standing before me who was about to be a dad. I moved in and gave him a quick hug, patting his back a couple of times before stepping back and grabbing his shoulder. I gave it a firm shake. "It's my turn to tell you to get out of your own head. This is great news, Spence. Congratulations, man. I'm really happy for you."

"Thanks," he replied, his breath coming out ragged. "I guess it's just ... I see Finn and how he's like a real person that you have to worry about turning out right. And not messing him up. Sorry, I know you're still getting to know our dad, but in a lot of ways he messed me up, dude. I don't want to do that."

I looked over at Mike with Finn. He was still patiently helping Finn with his swing. I'd learned some of his faults and was sure there were more I still hadn't heard about, but it was all secondhand accounts from Spencer. And since I was a dad, I'd bet my perspective in regard to choices I made concerning Finn would be a lot different than Finn's perspective on them. Especially if he were looking back as an adult and trying to put together the pieces of his childhood memories. It was weird to identify more with our dad than with my brother—my peer—but parenthood changes things. And now Spencer would find that out for himself.

Besides, past mistakes aside, he was making a great effort to do better. And bringing it back to my own worries from only moments before, I could see that if I'd messed up by not getting Finn outside earlier, I was making up for it now. He wasn't ruined. And neither was Spencer.

I looked back at my brother and sighed. "Don't get ahead of yourself, Spencer. They all come out as babies. All you gotta do is change their butt, feed them, keep them warm and feeling safe. It's all pretty basic at first. Take it one diaper change at a time."

He nodded. "Okay. Then what?"

"Then, by the time stuff gets harder, like dealing with temper tantrums, you'll be so used to taking care of the kid and worrying about what's best for him that you'll just do it. You'll figure it out. Maybe with a lot of Googling things like 'how to reason with a two-year-old' and finding that you can't, you'll find what works for you and your own kid."

"Right."

"And after all of that," I continued, "when big feelings or life stuff comes, and he starts acting like a real person with real emotions, you'll know him so well that you'll be able to get through whatever happens. Plus, you'll have us. This family we have now. It's great. And we'll help each other out."

I was certain Spencer hated getting emotional as much as the next Marine, so we both looked away and didn't say anything else for a long moment while we watched Mike and Finn in the grass in front of us. Finally, the mood lifted when Mike didn't get out of the way fast enough and Finn nailed him in the chest with a wayward swing.

I cringed through my laughter. "What was that you were saying about Finn being a golfer?"

"Yeah, maybe not."

A kid ran up to Finn and started chatting with him, and since his dad was right behind him, I did the typical dad thing and headed over to say hi. When I came within earshot, the kid was turning to his dad and pointing at Finn over his shoulder.

"This is the loser I told you about who always freaks out in PE."

The hairs on the back of my neck stood up. Who was this little twerp? "What's up, Finn?"

Finn's eyes were round as saucers as he looked between me and the kid. "Nothing."

"Hey, I'm Owen," I said to the dad, extending my hand.

He shook my hand. "I'm Brett. This is my son, Braydon. We just moved here a couple weeks ago, and I guess the boys have PE together."

I could tell by Finn's expression that he didn't want me to make a scene. "Great. Welcome to Miramar. See you around."

I gave the dad a dismissive wave and an expression that I knew was less than friendly. Even though Finn didn't want me to do anything about this bratty kid, I had to make sure Brett knew I'd heard what Braydon had said. Message received, Brett pulled his son by the shoulders, and they moved along.

Meeting Mike's eyes, I saw that he'd also overheard what the kid had said. I bent down to Finn's level. "What's up with that kid, bud?"

He wouldn't meet my gaze. "Nothing."

"Sounded like more than nothing."

"It's not." Finn looked at me then, and his eyes were filled with tears. "Can we go home now? I suck at playing golf."

Before I could say something about him not saying stuff like that, he threw the golf club in the grass between us and ran for the parking lot.

16

RACHEL

I wasn't watching where I was going when I left my office and ran right into Owen standing by the wall.

"Owen," I huffed, my hand on my heart. "You scared me."

"Sorry."

"Everything okay? Where's Finn?"

He gestured behind him. "My mom picked him up. We've had a bit of a day ... I came to see you."

Alarm bells went off in my head, but I tried to keep my cool. I pointed with my keys toward the parking lot. "My Jeep's over there if you want to sit and talk."

"Sounds good," he replied, holding his arm out for me to lead the way.

We walked in tense silence for a moment, but as we

reached the Jeep, I couldn't take it anymore. "Owen, hurry up and tell me what's going on. You're making me nervous."

We hopped into the open-air Jeep, and I couldn't take my eyes from his face. He didn't look like he was about to break up with me, though I wasn't exactly sure what that would look like. Would he be all teary? Angry? He was neither. He was ... nervous. Oh shoot, he'd probably be nervous if he were going to break up with me. I'd been nervous when I'd told him I didn't want to date my student's dad. A concept that I should have stuck with since it would have meant I wouldn't be sitting here with him now, about to get my dang heart broken.

"Couple things," he started. "First, is Finn having some trouble with a bully?"

I wrinkled my nose. Ugh. This wasn't even close to what I was worried about. But it was almost worse because Finn had specifically told me not to tell Owen about his issues with our newest transfer student, Braydon. And he asked me as his teacher, not his dad's girlfriend, who hoped to one day be his stepmom. Yeah, maybe it was presumptuous to go there, but I couldn't help it. Every time I looked at the guy, I wanted him to wife me up.

"Why do you ask?" I avoided his eyes and took down my ponytail, combing my fingers through my hair and then working it back up and into the hold of the elastic again.

"Because we ran into this kid at the golf course last night with my dad and Spencer and he gave me the bully vibe. Finn was pretty upset about it, but he wouldn't talk to me. The kid's dad said they had PE together."

I swallowed. "I will definitely keep my eye out and let you know."

It wasn't a lie. I would keep my eye out. And I would let him know. If I needed to. But unless something happened that he needed to know, I simply didn't want to break Finn's trust in me by telling him anything about Braydon. Nothing had happened yet other than the usual violations of Finn's rules of life. Braydon didn't play fair. Braydon didn't speak kindly. Braydon didn't follow instructions. It was nothing Owen needed to know about badly enough for me to get in trouble with Finn. Trust was hard to earn back once you'd lost it.

"Okay, thanks," he said. "I didn't want to push him. I figure he'll tell me when he's ready."

"For sure. What's the second thing?"

He blew out a breath and rubbed his hands down the front of his thighs. "Remember all that stuff I told you about moving from Station to Detachment?"

"Yeah." My throat was tight, so I cleared it, then spoke again. "Yes."

"I'm getting moved to Detachment."

"Which means you're deploying?" I guessed.

He nodded. "Yeah. First, I have to get all of my quals and all that other stuff I told you about. There are some smaller trips for me to do that before the bigger deployment. They're called 'dets.'"

"Dets?" My brain spun.

"For detachments."

I often used humor when I was nervous or upset. "Does that mean you call a deployment a 'dep'?"

He chuckled. "No."

I made a popping sound with my lips. "Worth a shot."

"Rach." He reached over and ran his fingers through my ponytail, making the hair on the back of my neck stand up. "You okay?"

I turned my head and pressed my cheek into his hand. "How long until you leave?"

"Six months."

I remembered him telling me about smaller training things they had to do before they left on the big deployment. "And how long of that six months will you be gone?"

He sucked in a breath, looking up to do the math. "Off and on, maybe half of that?"

It felt like all of the wind had been knocked out of me. I'd known he was a Marine from the very start. It wasn't until our date that I'd found out he'd never deployed, but even then, he told me up-front that it was a possibility in the future. But still, I couldn't help the feeling that it was coming out of left field.

A thought occurred to me and I reached over and squeezed his arm. "Finn."

"Finn."

We looked at each other, so many things crossing between us in the silence. I saw the fear swimming in his eyes, and as upset as I was for myself, my sole focus was on how it would affect Finn. And though I knew him as a strong and disciplined man, could Owen's heart handle leaving Finn after everything they'd been through?

I pulled my leg up in my seat and turned to face him, reaching out and grabbing the back of his neck. My forehead pressed to his, I looked deep into his eyes. "It's going to be okay."

He closed his eyes.

"Owen," I whispered, gently squeezing his neck. "Look at me."

His eyes opened slowly and met mine, wet with the tears he was apparently trying hard to keep from over-flowing.

I took a steadying breath. I couldn't allow my voice

to falter. "I've got Finn. I promise. Everything will be okay. Between me and your mom and Spencer and Ellie and Mike—even Noah and the rest of the friends. We're all a big family, and we'll take good care of him."

He swallowed, then angled his face forward and planted a fierce kiss on my lips. I kissed him back, trying to put all of the promises I'd made into the kiss. Was I upset? Yes. Did I want him to go? Heck no. But the love I felt for this father and son meant nothing could keep me from standing by them during this deployment.

The next few days went by in a blur. Finn took the news of the deployment better than I'd thought he would. We'd softened the blow by taking him out on a drive up the coast, sticking to the highway that ran parallel to the shore. It was a relaxing day, Owen looking handsome as ever while driving my jeep, the wind blowing in our hair.

We'd also gone to the Halloween store to pick out a trio of costumes. Finn thought it would be hilarious if he was a shark—pun intended—and Owen and I were an attack victim and a lifeguard. We bought the costumes and gave him credit for his silliness, even as I said his choice would probably prevent me from swimming the next time we all went to the beach. This, of course, led to an earful about shark attack statistics and their actual food preferences that lasted the entire ride home.

On Monday at school, I was practically on a high of lovesick happiness by the time Finn's fourth period class came around. So happy that I was literally singing Disney songs to myself as I supervised the kids running around the track. Then, unusual movement caught my eye at the other side of the gym, and the cheerful lyrics died on my lips.

"*Hey*," I called across the gym, white hot rage burning within me. "*Let him go.*"

My feet carried me swiftly from one end of the basketball court to the other, my eyes locked on the bully who had Finn pinned up against the safety padding behind the hoop. When I reached them, the other kids who'd gathered around dispersed, holding their hands out to signal that they had nothing to do with the scuffle between the two boys.

As a teacher, you absolutely *cannot* put hands on a student. In many cases, this is even true when there's a fight in progress. My limbs twitched at my sides with the urge to grab Braydon and push him away from Finn, but I knew I had to give him the opportunity to let him go before I tried to physically remove his hands from Finn's shoulders.

"Braydon," I seethed. "I'm only going to say this one more time. Get your hands *off* of him."

"Or what? You're going to tell his dad? Your *boyfriend*?"

His words hit me like a slap. My eyes flew to Finn's, finding so much hurt and anger there. This was all my fault. If I hadn't given in to Owen O'Malley and his freaking baby-blue eyes, Finn wouldn't be pinned against a wall getting bullied.

"What's the matter, Finn? When your daddy deploys, you'll have your new mommy here to take care of you. Don't you think she's tough enough?"

"Braydon Jeffries, if you don't let go of him this instant, I'm going to have to *make* you let go." I turned to one of the other students who I knew was responsible enough for the task. "Run to the office and tell Principal Hawthorne to come here. *Go!*"

With a smirk, Braydon turned back to Finn. "This kid is nothing but a wimp. You're only nice to him because you're his new mommy. Where is your real mommy, anyway, *Finnigan*? I don't see her anywhere. Oh yeah, that's right, she's—"

Before he could finish whatever nasty thing he was about to say, Finn wound up and walloped Braydon with a right hook I was sure the pudgy bully hadn't seen coming. The move sent the side of Braydon's face rocketing away from Finn's fist, but he still didn't break his hold on Finn's shoulders against the wall.

Hoping to stop Finn from getting hit back, I took one arm and brought it down on Braydon's forearms, removing his hands from Finn's shoulders with the least amount of physical contact that I could muster. Then, I moved my body to stand between them, looking him square in the face before glancing around to the other students to take their mood temperature. Everyone was very still, looking worriedly between me and Braydon. This was never a good situation for a teacher to be in. Teacher versus student was our worst nightmare. I prayed Principal Hawthorne would arrive soon.

Braydon smirked again. I wished more than anything that I could literally wipe that smile off his face with a Lysol wipe. Exhibiting an award-winning level of restraint, I held my hands out in front of me to keep them visible when the principal entered the gym.

"What's going on?" Principal Hawthorne bellowed as he entered the gym from the closest door. "Braydon Jeffries, back away."

Until he said that and Braydon stepped back, I hadn't registered how closely the nine-year-old had actually been standing to me. Braydon was one of those extremely tall and big-boned kids who skewed the scales as an outlier for average height and weight for this grade. Since I was on the petite side with a small frame and a height of five foot one, we were nearly eye to eye. I knew he wouldn't be a threat to me like an adult male might be, but still. My heart raced and adrenaline coursed through me.

"Are you okay, Ms. Peters?" Principal Hawthorne asked me, and then, as I stepped aside, he turned to Finn. "And how about you, Finn?"

We both answered that we were fine, and I fought the urge to pull him into a hug. I wanted to. Oh, how I wanted to. But I was already feeling like a terrible person for putting him in this position, and I didn't know how he'd react.

With the utmost level of professionalism, I calmly and evenly explained that the children had been doing laps around the gym when I looked up and saw Braydon pinning Finn to the wall. Then, because I knew I had to remain objective, I explained that Finn had punched Braydon after Braydon taunted him about his mom. I used as few adjectives as possible. I was trying to be professional, but it was hard to keep the emotion out of it.

My gaze raked over Finn, searching him for injuries. Thankfully, he'd been held against the safety padding on the wall and not the brick itself. There wasn't a scratch on him. Braydon, on the other hand, had a red mark on his cheekbone that I was sure wouldn't look pretty tomorrow.

Principal Hawthorne looked around. "I'll call Mrs. Evans to finish your class. Let's take this to my office."

With a nod, I held out my hand for Finn to go ahead and I followed behind him, keeping myself protectively between him and Braydon. When we got to the principal's office, Braydon went directly into a conference room with an aide while Principal Hawthorne called his parents. Owen would be the next call on his list, so I sat with Finn while we waited.

"Are you going to call my dad before the principal does?" Finn asked, not looking at me.

I shook my head. "No. That wouldn't be my place. He's going to call him in a minute."

Finn continued to stare blankly ahead. I wanted to pull him into my lap and hold him until his frown turned into the smile I was used to. I wanted to tell him a joke or a funny story to make his eyes light up. But I couldn't tell if his sullen expression was just because of Braydon's bullying or if it was also because my new place in his life might have caused it. And even worse, I knew that Finn had likely never punched anyone in his entire life. I wanted to help him process it.

After a few moments, I couldn't take it anymore. "Finn, please talk to me. Are you okay?"

"No."

"What started that? Last I saw, you guys were doing laps."

"Let's just wait for my dad."

I swallowed, then sat back in my chair. "Okay, that's fine."

A moment later, Principal Hawthorne stuck his head out of his door. "Ms. Peters, can you come in here please?"

I nodded, looking up to the secretary. "Will you keep an eye on him?"

"Of course," Pat replied.

"Thanks."

I tried to give Finn a reassuring smile, but he still wouldn't look at me. My heart sank as I got up and followed Principal Hawthorne into his office.

"Have a seat," he directed me as he closed the door behind us.

I took a seat in one of the two chairs before his desk and squared my shoulders. He sat down across from me and folded his hands on his desk. "I just got off the phone with both parents. They're on their way."

"Good," I replied, my heart squeezing at the thought of Owen being worried about Finn and rushing over here from work.

"The thing is, Mr. Jeffries told me some things I want to make you aware of."

I swallowed. "Yes?"

"He said Braydon has been complaining that Finn

gets special treatment in PE because you're dating his father. Is that true?"

The figurative rain cloud over my head opened up and dumped a gallon of water over my head. I stuttered out a reply, but nothing came out right.

"Ms. Peters," he went on, "I know this is your first year here, and I'm sure you know there is no official policy stating that parents and teachers cannot have a relationship. But the *appropriateness* of such a relationship is in question here. Are you in a romantic relationship with Finn's father?"

"Yes."

He sat back in his chair, sighing heavily. "And do you feel like you've been able to treat Finn the same as the rest of the students? Mr. Jeffries alleges that Finn gets to stand on the sidelines and talk to you while the rest of the class is doing the activities of the day. Apparently, Braydon doesn't think it's fair that Finn doesn't have to participate."

I fought the urge to roll my eyes. "Finn is hesitant about many physical activities, and since I'm trying to inspire a love of being active in him, I'm trying an approach that eases him in. Besides, after everything he's been through with losing his mom, he just needs some patience and understanding. He's made great progress in the two months or so that I've had him in class. I'm really impressed."

"I see. Well, it certainly sounds like you care about him a great deal."

"I do," I said through clenched teeth. "But I care about all of my students a great deal. Sara Rodriguez is afraid of heights, so I don't force her to climb the rope in my sixth-grade class. Daniel Carpenter doesn't know how to follow directions, but I'm actively trying to teach him how instead of always giving him detention like his homeroom teacher does. Cody Robbins couldn't tie his shoes at the beginning of the year and his parents were apparently too busy to teach him, so I spent five minutes with him every day after class until he learned how."

Principal Hawthorne's eyebrows ticked up and he removed his glasses. "I see."

"I hope you *see* that I care about all of my students the same way, whether I have a relationship with their dad or not."

"I do think you're a caring teacher, Ms. Peters. But I hope you'll reconsider this relationship, all the same. This is the first I've heard of it, but if other parents or students come forward, we're going to have to have another conversation about it. Besides, this altercation today may have been avoided if it weren't for the relationship, correct?"

Instantly triggered by his words, my eyes stung with tears. This was exactly how it had happened back in

Texas. That conniving ex-wife would convince another parent to come forward and complain about our relationship, and I'd be brought into the principal's office like a student in need of discipline and we'd have an awkward conversation just like this one. I'd hear all about how they didn't have an official policy but that it was apparently distracting to the students and detrimental to the community as a whole. Blah blah blah. I'd had enough embarrassing conversations like that to last me a lifetime.

What a ridiculous hill to die on, when it hadn't even worked out between us. I'd be a fool to go down that road again and make myself feel like a less-than-amazing teacher, even for a chance at love. I'd taken enough chances on love that hadn't worked out. What made me think this time would be any different? I could be there for Finn while Owen deployed as his teacher, even if we weren't together romantically. Couldn't I?

A knock sounded at the door and Pat from the front desk popped her head in. "Excuse me, sir. Both parents have arrived."

"Thank you," Principal Hawthorne replied. "Send them all in, please. Right, Ms. Peters? We're done here?"

"Yes, sir."

17

OWEN

Finn blasted out of the car the moment it came to a stop in the driveway. I barely remembered to put it in park before taking the key out and slamming the door behind me. "Finn!"

He ignored me and dashed into the house, leaving the front door wide open behind him. Smart kid. If he'd slammed it in my face, we'd have a problem.

My mom met me at the door. "What's going on? Why isn't he at school still?"

"He got in a fight," I explained with a sigh. I started to follow him upstairs, then put my hand on the rail and hung my head. What would I even say? I needed a minute. Pushing off from the stairs I headed to the kitchen instead, dropping into a chair.

"He got in a fight." She said it like a statement,

almost as if she were trying to process it. "Finn. Our Finn. Got in a fight."

I nodded. "Yep."

"With whom?"

"This kid Braydon. We actually ran into him and his dad at the golf course, do you remember? That kid I told you called him a loser?"

She rolled her eyes. "Yes. It took forever to get him to come out of his room that night. I didn't realize it was still a problem. He hasn't brought it up again."

"I know. And I've asked him about it a couple of times but he says he doesn't talk to the kid. And, what's worse, is that I asked Rachel about him. And she lied to me."

Mom dropped into the chair across from me. "Okay, let's back up. Start from the beginning with the fight."

"So, according to *Rachel*, the kids were running laps in the gym. She looked up and Braydon had Finn pinned against the wall. She went over to break it up, and Braydon said something to her about me being her boyfriend. Then, he said something about the deployment and Rebecca. I don't remember the exact words, but whatever is was, Finn punched him."

Her hands flew up and covered her mouth. "He didn't."

"He did. And apparently Rachel hadn't even gotten

the kid to let go of him yet so he was able to hit him while he was still pinned up against the wall."

"Is that supposed to be impressive?"

"I mean, I'm impressed."

She rolled her eyes. "Don't tell him that."

"Look, I know fighting isn't the answer. I'm not going to condone it. I'm just saying, he's scared of a lot of stuff and this isn't the first time he's been bullied. I'm glad he didn't let that kid say something about Rebecca and get away with it. Besides, he was being restrained against a wall. I'm glad he tried to fight back."

Mom sighed heavily. "Rachel broke it up before Finn could get hurt, right?"

"Oh, yeah, yeah. The kid wasn't able to hit him back or anything, thankfully." I scratched my head. "I can't believe my kid got in a fight. Didn't see myself getting *that* phone call today."

"Have you gotten a chance to talk to him about it? He needs to know it's not okay to haul off and punch someone just because you don't like what they're saying."

I shook my head. "Not yet. He wouldn't talk to me in the car, and I wanted to wait until we got home so I could give him some time. Well, also to give myself some time. I'm having a hard time figuring out what to say. I mean, again, I'm glad he wasn't scared of the kid."

"What did you mean about Rachel lying to you about the bully?"

A knock sounded at the door and we both looked up with a start. Mom frowned. "Who could that be?"

"I'll get it," I said, crossing through the kitchen and opening the door. "Rachel."

"Hey."

"What's up? I thought we were going to meet up later."

Everything had been so tense at the school that we hadn't had a chance to talk. Between hearing the fight story, trying to talk to Finn about his suspension, and listening to the principal counsel the other family about the bullying from their son, there just hadn't been an opportunity to be alone. Truthfully, I was glad. Because I was pretty heated about the fact that she'd lied to me when I asked about Braydon. I didn't know what to say to her, either.

"I know, and I'm sorry. I'm sure you have your hands full with Finn. But I really need to talk to you, and I couldn't wait."

I stepped back and opened the door wider. "Come on in."

"Hey, Rachel," my mom greeted her as we walked into the kitchen. Then her face changed after studying Rachel's, and she stood from her seat. "I'm gonna let you guys talk. I'll be upstairs if you need me."

"Thanks, Mom." I watched her go, but there was a sinking feeling in my gut like she was abandoning me to deal with something hard all by myself. I shook my head and focused back on Rachel. "So, what did you want to talk about?"

Rachel worried her hands in front of her. "Owen. The principal called me into his office before you got there and told me the other parents filed a complaint about us being together."

"I figured. They brought up the same thing after you left. I just told them you didn't give him any special treatment and to mind their own business."

She frowned. "What did Principal Hawthorne say?"

"He said he strongly discouraged parents having a relationship with their child's teacher. I told him I didn't think it was right to talk about it in front of the kids like I was one of his students getting in trouble."

"Are you serious?"

"What? He was being condescending."

"Owen. That's my boss."

"Okay, well your boss was being a jerk. In front of my kid and the kid who was bullying him. Not exactly the right impression to make."

She sighed and took out her ponytail, combed her fingers through her hair, then neatly wrapped the hair tie back around it on top of her head. "Owen, I'm sorry. I don't think I can do this."

"Do what?"

"Date my student's father. *Again.*" She put her hands on her hips. "You weren't there today when Braydon taunted Finn about you being my boyfriend or whatever. He said something about how he would only have me and not you. Finn looked so hurt and he was in that position just because we decided to start dating."

I rolled my eyes. "That is not why he was in that position. And if he doesn't know it, we'll just tell him."

"Oh, sure. If that kid didn't single him out because we're dating, why did he?"

"I can't explain to you the inner workings of a bully's mind, Rachel. He sucks. He called Finn a loser when we saw him on the golf course, he taunted him about us, he was about to say something about his mom. It is what it is. But I'm glad Finn stood up for himself."

Her eyes bulged. "Owen. Seriously, you did not just say you're glad your son punched another student."

I held out my hands. "This is hard for me, Rach. I'm a dad. Any dad would be proud to hear their son didn't let a bully get the best of him. He was pinned to a freaking wall."

"I know he was pinned to a freaking wall. But his *teacher* was right there, trying to handle the situation. He should have let me use my words to de-escalate the situation."

"Oh, right, right. And how well did your words de-escalate the situation leading up to this point? Last week at the golf course he called Finn a loser. You can't tell me you haven't noticed anything happening in class. I point-blank asked you if there was something going on."

"I have been handling it."

I crossed my arms. "Handling it how?"

"I've separated them on multiple occasions, I've talked to both of them after class, I make sure they're not in the same groups during activities—"

I felt anger swell within me. "Wow. I didn't realize it was such an issue. And you didn't think you needed to discuss it with me? Even when I asked you about it?"

"If I told every parent about every situation like that, I'd be on the phone with them constantly. It's PE. The kids get wild, tempers flare. I had it under control."

I scoffed. "Clearly."

"Owen O'Malley," she said, jabbing a finger in my direction, "this is exactly what I was worried about. We are on two sides of Finn's life. This is not good for either of us. I can't give you special treatment just because we're dating. Like I said, I wouldn't call anybody else's parents until I'd handled it myself. Why would I do it for you?"

I threw up my hands. "Because it's not like you have to make a special effort to call me, Rach. We'd already be sitting across the table from each other at dinner."

"That's my point."

"Mine too."

She sighed. "Just promise me you won't try to tell him it's okay that he punched Braydon."

I blinked at her. "You're trying to tell me what to say to my son?"

"As a teacher, I need to remain objective. I can't condone Finn *punching* another student. Two people in a relationship should be able to be united in these kinds of parenting situations. We aren't able to do that because you're the classic dad who's proud of his son for punching out a bully."

"Fine. I'm not going to tell him it's okay to punch people. *Okay*? I'm smart enough to know that's not good parenting. But the kid had him pinned against a wall, and he was about to say something about his mom, so he punched him. I can think of a hundred worse reasons to punch someone."

Rachel put her hands on her head. "Oh my goodness, we are talking in circles right now. I can't do this."

"I still can't believe you never told me this was an issue. When I go on a det or on deployment, I need to know you're going to tell me what's going on with my son. Not lie to me about it."

"I didn't lie to you. You can't get special treatment," she clapped her hands with each syllable of the sentence. "Telling you about Braydon over dinner is crossing a professional line. I was handling it in the classroom while it was still contained in the classroom. Today, it blew up."

"I'll say."

"Do you see what I'm saying now? Do you see how sticky this is? If I was just a teacher at the school but didn't teach your son, it would be fine. If you were just a parent, but not of one of my students, that would be fine. But this ... not being able to be on the same side of a situation and see eye to eye on it, it's never going to work. And I'm sorry, but you're not in the classroom with them. Finn got targeted by Braydon because of the special attention I give him. And I really think it's because I care about Finn, and not so much because I'm with you. But either way, it's not good for anyone, and it needs to stop."

I backed up and leaned against the wall behind me, arms still crossed over my chest. "Fine, if that's what you want. You're his teacher, I'm his dad. I'll handle this punching thing as I see fit, and you do your best to keep that kid away from my son when I'm gone."

"Fine."

And with that, she spun on her heel and left.

18

RACHEL

"You know the way he feels about the bully thing is totally normal for a dad, right?" Ivy asked, her face leaving the video chat screen for a second as she leaned over to take a bite of her sandwich.

"I'm sure it is. I've never been a dad before." I sat back in my chair in the teacher's lounge, grateful that even with the two-hour time difference between California and Texas, Ivy and I were able to connect on my lunch break and her prep period.

Ivy lifted a brow. "Rach. If you weren't Finn's teacher, you know you'd be proud of him for standing up for himself."

"But I *am* Finn's teacher. That's the point of all of this. He shouldn't be taught that it's okay to hit people.

That's absurd. If Owen thinks that's okay to teach him, I don't want any part of it. Maybe we're not compatible after all."

"Did Owen *say* he was going to tell him it was okay to hit that kid?"

I bit my lip. "No."

"All I'm saying is it's a normal feeling for the dad to be like, 'Yeah, son, don't let them push you around.' You know?"

I couldn't help but laugh at her impression of a tough dad with a low voice, flexing his muscles. "I guess. Ugh, it's just all so complicated."

"It seems to me that you're the one complicating it. I'm sorry, don't look at me like that. I know you better than anyone, and I've watched you go through so many guys, holding them to these impossibly high standards, and ending it for reasons that didn't make sense to me. I'm giving you tough love because you left home to start fresh. San Diego is your home now. Owen and Finn could be your home. But instead, you're holding on to the past and letting it get in the way. Again."

My eyes filled up with tears. "That is harsh, friend."

"I know. And I'm sorry. But Rachel, listen to me. First of all, just know that I love you and everything I'm about to say is coming from a place of love. Okay?"

I nodded at my phone, unable to verbally reply. Tough love from Ivy was a necessary evil in my life. I'd missed it while living in San Diego the last few months. And whether I wanted to admit it or not, I needed her to fix this.

Ivy brought the phone closer to her face. "Don't forget that I dated one guy for so long that when we finally broke up, I didn't even know who I was without him. Then when I met Jake—and you know, you saw— he was so different from Cory that comparisons rarely came up. But *you* love to date. And that's not a bad thing. You go, girl. But that means you have a longer list of guys to compare each guy to. And each and every time you were about to get close to someone, you'd pull up some 'thing' that happened in the past with one ex or another, and boom. It was over. This time, it happens to be that one time you dated a dad and things were dramatic. I was there, I get it. It was rough. But if you'd met a cute fireman out there in San Diego, who do you think you'd have compared him to?"

I chuckled, tears running down my face, remembering the one firefighter I'd dated who had a tendency to lie. "Bobby."

"Exactly. Bobby," Ivy confirmed. "And if you'd met a cute mechanic?"

"Allen."

"Mm-hmm. Should I go on?"

I sniffed, wiping my nose with my napkin. "No, I

already sound like I've been around the block one too many times."

"Aw, friend," Ivy crooned, "I'm not trying to make you feel like that. I know you're a hopeless romantic, and you're always looking for the right guy. I'm not trying to make you feel bad. I'm just saying that you can't hold these guys up to impossible standards, and you can't run away as soon as the past catches up and reminds you it exists. Okay?"

"Okay."

"So, now what?" she asked.

I shrugged. "It doesn't matter now. We've been broken up for a week, and I haven't heard from him or seen him. Finn is so down in class, and every time I try to talk to him privately, he ignores me. There's only so much I can do before I'm crossing a line as his teacher, you know?"

Being that Ivy was also a teacher, she got it. "Yeah, for sure. He's not the one you need to chase down and force to talk to you."

"You think I should chase Owen down?" I asked, laughing despite myself. "I swear, Vee, this conversation is making me sound like a freak."

She laughed heartily. "Rach, the time you spent with Owen was the happiest I've ever seen you. You're good together, and the three of you as a family will work. You just need to let go of the past."

"All of this is well and good, but there's still the matter of my job."

Ivy waved a hand. "Girl, please. The last time you dealt with issues like this, the dude wasn't even worth it. But you pulled through and stayed at that school for *years* after he moved away. If you'd put up with annoying stuff with the administration for him, why wouldn't you put up with it for Owen and Finn? I'm sure any talk of inappropriateness will die down with time, just like most things in life. It's not gossip if everyone knows about it. It's not new and exciting if you've been together forever. You know?"

She was right. I knew she was. But it still stung to hear that all of these things I'd been so sure about were just roadblocks of my own creation, designed to push Owen away. I put my head in my hands, the phone propped up on the water bottle in front of me.

"I'm a mess. Now we have this deployment looming. What if there's not enough time to make things right? What if he doesn't forgive me for freaking out and ending things? After everything he and Finn have been through with losing Rebecca ... and now Finn won't talk to me and it's my fault he's hurting. Again."

"There's only one way to find out. When's the next time you're going to see him?"

I bit my lip. "The Halloween party at baseball practice tomorrow."

"When he sees you in that *Baywatch* costume, I'm sure he'll be a goner."

"It's a Halloween party with the team, Vee. I'm not going full *Baywatch.*"

She waved a hand. "I'm sure he has a good enough imagination."

"Finn, can we talk?"

He turned around in his desk chair, his face sullen. "Talk about what?"

"Talk about the fight. Rachel. All of it."

"We've already talked about the fight. I get it, don't hit. Violence isn't the answer. *Blah blah blah.*"

I took a step into his room and sat on the bed across from him. "Finn, come on. I've talked at you about the fight, but we haven't talked about it in a back-and-forth conversation kind of way. Do you know what I mean?"

"What do you want me to say? I already said I'm sorry I hit him. You already told me not to do it again."

I scratched my head. "I know, it's just. It's a bigger, more complicated thing than we've dealt with in a while, and I just want to make sure we're on the same page. Okay?"

He nodded. "Fine."

"So, how has it been with Braydon at school since the fight?"

"Fine. He doesn't talk to me anymore. And he doesn't push me when he walks by me."

Relief swam within me. I'd worried that the kid would be meaner to him in the days following the incident, but it sounded like the opposite was true. Fighting still wasn't the answer, but maybe Finn's right hook had gotten the kid to realize he wasn't one to mess with. I shook my head, scolding myself. Parenting was hard.

"And, um, how are things going in PE otherwise?"

"You mean how is it with *Rachel*? I mean ... Ms. Peters."

I nodded. "Yeah. How's that?"

"I don't talk to her."

"Why?"

"Because she bailed on us. I didn't think she would. I thought that once I got you guys together, she'd stick around. But she didn't. And I hate that I have to see her every day and get reminded of it. I liked her a lot."

My heart hurt. I'd always known Finn was bright and that he experienced his feelings very profoundly, but his articulate nature meant that when he was having deep feelings, they were always a kick in the gut. "I'm sorry, bud."

"You didn't try very hard to stop her from bailing, you know."

"What?"

"I heard you guys fighting in the kitchen. You let her walk out."

I leaned forward. "Finn, it's not like I could make her stay."

"I wish you could have made Mom stay," he mumbled the words so low I barely heard them, but that didn't make them hurt any less. He looked up at me and must have seen how his words affected me because he shook his head rapidly. "I'm sorry."

"It's okay," I whispered. "I wish I could have made Mom stay, too."

The silence hung in the air around us for a long moment, then finally he looked up. "Do you wish you could have made Rachel stay?"

"I mean, I wish I'd known what to say at the time that would have convinced her not to break up with me. But I didn't. I was pretty frustrated that day, too."

"I heard. You said you were mad she didn't tell you Braydon was being mean to me. And that you didn't want to worry about that while you were gone on deployment."

I nodded. "Yeah. I know I can trust Grandma and even Grandpa Mike and Uncle Spencer. But I wanted to be able to trust her, too."

"Yeah well, I trust her."

"Finn."

"I asked her not to tell you. And she didn't."

My gaze searched his. She hadn't wanted to cross the line between his trust in her and her relationship with me. "You did?"

"Yeah. I didn't want you to think I was a wuss or I couldn't handle it. Because I could. I just ignored him. But then that day he was so mean, he wanted me to give him my lunch card. And I said no. So that's why he pushed me up against the wall."

I leaned back. Kids were still beating up other kids over lunch money? What a trip. "Why didn't you tell anyone that when they asked how it all started?"

He shrugged. "Because if I'd just given it to him in the first place none of this would have happened. Everything would be normal and I wouldn't have gotten suspended for two days."

"Finn, buddy, you did the right thing by saying no. He doesn't get to take your lunch money just because you're afraid of what might happen if you say no."

"I guess."

"This whole thing was a mess. I wish your mom

were here to help us through it. I know she'd know what to do."

"Me too."

I let the silence hang for a minute, thinking hard about my words before I let them out. "But since she's not here, and you have me, just do me a favor and promise that you won't keep something like that from me again, okay? Maybe I could have gotten involved before it got to that point, you know? I'm glad you thought you could trust Rachel. But I also want you to feel like you can trust me with stuff like this. I'm always going to be in your corner."

He squared his shoulders. "Rach—I mean, Ms. Peters—was helping me. And she stepped in to do something about it."

"Right, but then you wound up punching the kid. And that's not okay."

"I could tell the stuff he was saying made her sad. She didn't like it."

I scratched my head. "Yeah, he was about to say something about your mom being gone, right?"

"Yeah, and he also said something about me only having her while you were on deployment, which I was fine with, but maybe she's scared about it. He just needed to stop talking."

"Uh, wait. Lemme get this straight." I held up a

finger. "You punched him because you didn't want him to say something else that would upset Rachel?"

Finn nodded. "Grandma says Mom is always watching me from Heaven. I know she loves me even though she's not here, and I bet she loves Rachel, too. I didn't want Braydon to make her sad and ruin it. But either way, it's ruined now. So, nothing I did was right. And none of it matters."

So many emotions flooded me in that moment, not the least of which was the urge to laugh at his dramatic flair. He could give any emo kid with black hair and nail polish a run for their money in that moment.

I sighed loudly and rustled his hair. "What am I going to do with you?"

"As long as it isn't golf, I don't care."

We laughed together, and I found myself saying a quick prayer of thanks that this rough conversation might have been the breakthrough we needed to start to get back to normal.

"Hey, Dad?"

"Yeah, bud?"

"Can you tell Rachel, I mean, Ms. Peters, that you want her to be your girlfriend again? I know you do."

"Sounds so simple, but I'm not sure it is."

Finn shrugged. "Ms. Peters said everything can be solved with our words. Even big things. I think she was trying to tell me not to punch people anymore, but you could probably try using your words with her, too."

"Oh, you think?" I asked, raising a brow and poking him in the side.

"Yes," he replied, laughing.

"Fine. Let's tell her together at the Halloween party at practice tomorrow."

He brightened. "Are we still going to wear our costumes we picked out?"

"Did you buy another one I don't know about?"

"No."

"Then yes, we'll have to wear those ones."

"Do you think she'll be wearing her lifeguard one so she's part of our costume trio again?"

I put an arm around his shoulders. "I hope so, bud. Also, it'll be good to get you back out there on the field. Don't think Grandma didn't tell me that you skipped practice all week while I was on night crew."

Finn looked rightfully abashed. "Sorry. I just didn't want to see her again. It makes me sad. But I can't skip PE 'cause they'd call you."

"Oh, Finn. I love you."

He beamed. "I love you, too."

"Well if it isn't Finn the Shark and his latest victim," Rachel greeted us, wearing a lifeguard uniform with shorts and holding a baseball bat. "I wasn't sure if you were still on the team, bud. You missed practice all week."

Finn dug the toe of his cleat into the dirt. "I know, I'm sorry. But I wouldn't miss the Halloween party."

"Were you on nights?" she asked me.

"Yeah, my mom let him stay home."

"Ah," she said, eyeing him carefully. "You look great in your costume, Finn."

"Thanks. You too."

"Did you decide to stop avoiding me?" she asked.

Finn blushed. "Yes, ma'am."

"Good," she said. "I've missed you."

"I've missed you, too," he said, jumping into her arms and hugging her tight around the waist.

He stepped back and looked around. "Are we going to play baseball in our costumes?"

"No, it's just tag and snacks for the party, bud," I replied. "You can go head over there where Noah is if you want something to eat."

Finn looked through the opening in his giant shark head at where Noah stood, waving a hand. Finn looked back at me. "What's he supposed to be?"

Rachel laughed. "He's Johnny Bravo."

"Who's that?"

"It's a cartoon character from when we were kids."

Finn wrinkled his nose. "Why would he want to be an ancient cartoon character?"

"Just go, Finn," I said, laughing even as I was losing my patience.

"Can you handle this by yourself?" he asked, peering up at me from under the shade of his pointy jaws.

"Uh, yeah, bud. Beat it." I turned back to Lifeguard Rachel with a laugh. "So, how've you been?"

"Fine."

"Did you miss me, too?"

"Maybe." Her smile was slow, but it was real. "Nice wounds."

I sniffed, looking down at my mangled arm and leg, impressed by how realistic Halloween gore was getting. "Thanks. Nice—well, you look amazing."

"Thanks."

I thoroughly enjoyed the blush that appeared on her cheeks and I had to work to keep my mind from going places it shouldn't go. "Finn told me you said everything can be solved if we use our words."

"Yeah, words. Not punching."

I held out my hands. "I know, no punching. He knows, too. But come on, you can't tell me you weren't a little bit proud of him for sticking up for himself."

She swatted my hand out of the air as I held my

pointer finger and thumb about a half an inch apart. "Hush, you. I will not admit to that."

"That's what I thought."

For a minute, we just stood there, smiling at each other and looking around awkwardly. Finn made a hissing sound so I turned to look at him and he made the motion of giving someone a hug, then gave me a thumbs up. I turned back to Rachel, and found her trying to hide a grin.

"Is he trying to tell you to hug me?"

I pursed my lips. "He said he always feels better after a hug."

"No PDA on base though, right?"

"We're allowed to hug."

She folded her arms over her chest, a subtle warning for me to keep my distance. "What's the deal, though, Owen? Are we just going to pretend like it isn't hard being a team for this kid when one of us is his teacher and the other is his parent? When you leave, you're right, you need to be able to trust me to have Finn's back but to also let you know what's going on with him. I'm confident that I'll be able to do that as his teacher, but being with you makes it messy."

"Look. I get that there need to be boundaries. I'm sorry I got mad at you for not telling me about the bullying. Finn told me he asked you not to tell me."

"He made me promise."

"I'm glad he can trust you." I looked over my shoulder at him, finding him doing a terrible job at pretending not to watch us while he hung out with Noah and his giant plastic hair. "He was eavesdropping when we were talking that day in the kitchen."

"Of course he was."

"He heard you keep your promise."

"Good."

"But, listen, as it stands right now, my mom is the one on the paperwork for the deployment. She's the one who is legally responsible for him while I'm gone. I'm not expecting you to just jump in here and be his mom right now. I know how big of a deal that is, and I'm not trying to drop the responsibility of all of that in your lap right away."

She looked over at him again, then back at me. "So, what are you asking?"

"I'm asking for a chance to get there. I know dating someone with a kid isn't casual. You're doing it knowing the goal is to join this family. So, I'm asking for the chance for us to try to get there."

"Fine. But when we're at school, I have to be Ms. Peters to him. I want him to trust me as an authority figure at school ..."

"And at home."

She blinked. "Yes, when we're together outside of school, too—"

"No, I don't just mean outside of school. I literally mean, *at home*." I took her hands in mine. "I want to marry you someday. I want that to be our future. Do you want that, too?"

"Yes," she replied, nodding. "I want that, too."

My shoulders straightened as an imaginary weight lifted off of them. "Good."

"I'm really sorry I freaked out," she continued. "I shouldn't have let my past bleed into what we had here."

I shook my head. "It's fine. I don't blame you. I know you had a bad experience before, and it kind of blew up in our faces there for a minute, but the moment I met you, I wanted to know you. And after I found out who you were, I couldn't shake the feeling that we were supposed to be in each other's lives. I just felt like we had something real. And watching you with my son has shown me that you love him just as much as I think you love me."

"I *do* love you," she said, her eyes wet with unshed tears.

"I love you, too." Since I'd pretty much poured out all of the words I could think of already, I reached for the bat in her hands and tossed it aside, pulling her into my arms and kissing her tenderly on the lips. San Diego may be where I'm living, but having her in my arms made me feel more at home than I had in years.

"*Shark attack*," came a fierce cry from behind her.

We broke apart just in time for Finn to crash into us. We let him take us down to the ground in a huge heap in the grass. Laughing, my little shark made chomping noises as he pretended to bite my fake-mangled arm. Rachel the lifeguard karate chopped the thick padding of his costume, trying to save me.

Little did she know, in some ways, she'd already saved us both.

EPILOGUE
NOAH

I thanked the cashier and took the shopping bag from her, pumped to show off my new jersey at the football party I was hosting tomorrow. When I turned to leave, a group of familiar faces walked by the entrance of the store.

I jogged forward and stepped into the sunlit corridor of the outdoor mall. "Hey, guys, wait up."

Hawkins, O'Malley, and his son, Finn, stopped and turned, Finn lighting up when he saw me. "Noah!"

"Hey, little man," I greeted him, then nodded at his dad and uncle. "What brings you guys to the mall?"

Hawk patted a nervous-looking O'Malley on the back. "Ring shopping."

"Ring shopping?" I asked, my eyes bulging. "For Rachel?"

"No, for Paige Walker," Hawk teased. "Of course, for Rachel."

I decided not to comment on him poking fun at me for what everyone assumed was a simple celebrity crush. Little did they know, it was so much more than that. Not that it mattered, since Paige was apparently determined to pretend that I didn't exist.

"My dad is going to ask Rachel to marry him at the Marine Corps ball next week," Finn explained, grinning from ear to ear.

O'Malley put an arm around his son. "That's the plan."

"I told him it wasn't very original, but he never listens to me," Hawk said.

I chuckled. "Didn't you propose at the ball one year?"

Hawk nodded. "Yep."

"Do you guys think that matters?" O'Malley asked. "I just figured because it was her first ball and it was romantic or whatever."

"You do you, or in this case, do me," Hawk said, "but I think you could be a little more creative. Even our dad has big plans for his proposal."

I held out my hands. "Wait, wait, Mike is proposing too?"

O'Malley gave Hawk a look, nodded at Finn as if he wasn't supposed to know, then turned back to me with a shake of his head. "He's planning to propose to my mom at Christmas. He came to me to ask for my blessing. And it was *supposed* to be a secret."

Finn waved a hand. "I knew before you did. I heard Uncle Spencer and Aunt Ellie talking about it when they were babysitting me. They thought I was sleeping."

We all laughed, completely unsurprised that the group's resident special agent had overheard the adults gossiping again. This kid was a master eavesdropper and knew everything about everyone. I liked to think of him as our version of neighborhood watch.

"Anyway, we're here to look at rings." O'Malley said. "I might still propose at the ball, but I'll give it some thought."

"You should take her on a dolphin tour. She wants to go on one," Finn offered.

O'Malley rustled Finn's hair. "Thanks for the tip, bud, I'll keep that in mind."

"What did you get?" Hawk asked me, gesturing to my shopping bag from the sports store I'd just left.

I pulled the jersey out of the bag and held it up. "It's for tomorrow. Will you guys be there?"

"Nice," O'Malley said, "and yes, all three of us will be."

Hawk scratched the back of his neck. "And, uh, the three of us will be there, too. I guess."

I tilted my head at him, confused. "The three of you?"

"Aunt Ellie's pregnant," Finn explained, again, with a mega-watt smile.

"Jeez, you guys," I dropped the jersey back in the bag and held my hand out for a congratulatory shake for Hawk. "Congrats, man. Wow. Anything else exciting going on around here? Am I the only one a million miles away from marriage and kids?"

Finn held up his small hand. "I'm with you."

Laughing, I gave him a high five. "Just me and you, kid."

"Don't worry, West," Hawk said, "I'm sure your time will come. You could always ask another celebrity to this year's ball. Don't let that stuff with Paige Walker keep you from trying for Jennifer Lawrence."

I rolled my eyes, again letting him think Paige was just any actress as far as I was concerned. "Yeah, yeah."

"Who's Jennifer Lawrence?" Finn asked.

"*Hunger Games*," O'Malley replied. "I'll let you watch it when you're a bit older. It's kind of dark."

Hawk waved a hand. "What, an arena full of children battling to the death is dark? Come on."

"Take it easy with the cool uncle routine or I'll take away your babysitting privileges," O'Malley warned his brother, making us laugh and Finn shake his head like that would be the worst thing ever.

"All right, I'll let you guys get back to your ring shopping," I said. "Congratulations on the baby, Hawk. And the engagement for you guys."

"Thanks, see you tomorrow," they all said their goodbyes and waved as they headed for the jewelry store.

I watched them go for a minute, shaking my head. O'Malley proposing to Rachel meant I was officially the last one in the group who was single. Shoot, even Mike proposing to O'Malley's mom took him out of my meager single club. It really was just me and the kid.

Sighing, I turned to head home. My watch buzzed with a social media notification, so I turned my wrist to read it, almost dropping the shopping bag when I read the words on the tiny screen.

@therealpaigewalker wants to send you a message

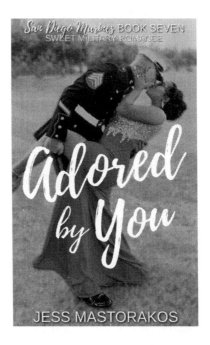

W anna find out what happens next for Noah and Paige? Visit http://jessmastorakos.com/ adored-by-you to grab your copy of the seventh and final book in the San Diego Marines series.

ALSO BY JESS MASTORAKOS

THE SAN DIEGO MARINES SERIES

Forever with You (Vince & Sara)

Back to You (Spencer & Ellie)

Away from You (Matt & Olivia)

Christmas with You (Cooper & Angie)

Believing in You (Jake & Ivy)

Memories of You (Brooks & Cat)

Home with You (Owen & Rachel)

Adored by You (Noah & Paige)

THE KAILUA MARINES SERIES

Coming soon!

CHRISTMAS IN SNOW HILL

A Movie Star for Christmas (Nick & Holly)

Christmas with the Boy Next Door (Jack and Robin)

ABOUT THE AUTHOR

Jess Mastorakos writes clean military romance books that feature heroes with heart and the strong women they love. She is a proud Marine wife and mama of four. She loves her coffee in a glitter tumbler and planning with an erasable pen.

instagram.com/author_jessmastorakos

bookbub.com/authors/jess-mastorakos

goodreads.com/author_jessmastorakos

SIGN UP FOR JESS'S SWEET ROMANCE SQUAD

Sign up for my newsletter at http://jessmastorakos.com/forever-with-you to get the free ebook version of Forever with You: A San Diego Marines Prequel. You'll also get bonus content, sweet romance book recommendations, and never miss a new release!

📷 instagram.com/author_jessmastorakos

BB bookbub.com/authors/jess-mastorakos

g goodreads.com/author_jessmastorakos